Praise for *Limbo, and Other Places I Have Lived*

"Each of Lily Tuck's short stories is a wonder of both craft and imagination. In sum, they constitute an exhilarating collection."

—George Plimpton

"Mesmerizing. . . . Tuck has a sharp eye for life's uncomfortable nuances."

—*Philadelphia Inquirer*

"This exquisite collection has a singular toughness, which comes from the author's frank, bold observations of the wayward heart. Tuck registers beauty and cruelty, refinement and vulgarity with equal force, until these opposites begin to merge like a spinning mandala. She is a wonderful writer, whose precision and inward acuity you can always trust."

—Philip Lopate

"Fourteen incisive yet intriguingly subtle tales of women in transition. . . . *[Limbo, and Other Places I Have Lived]* is a metaphysical adventure with richly uncommon observations that reveal uncertain emotions."

—*Booklist*

"The writing in Lily Tuck's *Limbo* is like a parachute flare that lights up a landscape with eerie precision—it's not just the places and people but the heroines' minds that are caught in this magnesium intensity. This is a terrific book of stories."

—John Casey

"[Lily Tuck is] an elegantly economical stylist able to evoke complex internal meltdowns with a simple stoke of the keys."

—*Hartford Courant*

Marion Ettlinger

About the Author

LILY TUCK was born in Paris and is the author of the novels *Interviewing Matisse, The Woman Who Walked on Water,* and *Siam*. Her short fiction has appeared in *The New Yorker, Fiction,* and *The Antioch Review*. She divides her time between Maine and New York City.

Limbo, and
Other Places
I Have Lived

Also by Lily Tuck

Interviewing Matisse, or The Woman Who Died Standing Up
The Woman Who Walked on Water
Siam, or The Woman Who Shot a Man

Limbo, and Other Places I Have Lived

short stories

Lily Tuck

Perennial
An Imprint of HarperCollins*Publishers*

"Hotter" and "La Mayonette" were originally published in *The New Yorker.*

A hardcover edition of this book was published in 2002 by HarperCollins Publishers.

First Perennial edition published 2003.

Designed by The Book Design Group / Matt Perry Ratto

The Library of Congress has catalogued the hardcover edition as follows:

Tuck, Lily.
Limbo, and other places I have lived / Lily Tuck.—1st ed.
p. cm.
ISBN 0-06-620942-0
1. Women—Fiction. I. Title.
PS3570.U236 L5 2002
813'.54—dc21

ISBN 0-06-093485-9 (pbk.)

04 05 06 07 ❖/RRD 10 9 8 7 6 5 4 3 2

In memory of my father, Rodolphe Solmsen,
and to Georges Borchardt

Acknowledgments

"Hotter" and "La Mayonette" appeared in *The New Yorker*; "The View from Madama Butterfly's House" appeared in *The American Voice*; "Gold Leaf," "Verdi," and "Limbo" appeared in *The Antioch Review*; "Horses" appeared in *Fiction*; "L'Esprit de L'Escalier" appeared in *The Paris Review*; "Second Wife" appeared in *Redbook*; "Ouarzazate" (published as Liliane Emery) appeared in *Willow Springs*; "Rue Guynemer" appeared in *Bomb*; and "Fortitude" and "Dream House" appeared in *Epoch*.

In the air, that's where your roots are, over there, in the air.

—Paul Celan

Contents

La Mayonette

We arrive at La Mayonette very late at night. My husband, Charles, and I had calculated eight hours for the drive but it took much longer since we did not take into account the winding part on the map between Geneva and Lyons—that part alone took five hours. Also, not realizing how far we still had to go, we had stopped along the way to have a picnic lunch and, lastly, just after it had got dark, the two bicycles that were attached, upside down, to the roof rack of the car worked themselves loose and we had to stop once more to reattach them. "If the bicycles fall off, someone could get hurt. Seriously hurt," I kept saying to Charles, as I tried to hold the flashlight steady and as he tried to tighten the bungee cords that held the bicycles down, and this, too, took up more time. Now, and for once uncomplaining, our two boys are huddled against each other in the back of the car asleep as we drive up to Francine's house to get the key to La Mayonette. We wake her up but she does not seem to mind. She was afraid, she tells us, that we had had an accident; she is relieved to see us. Her long hair is tied into a single old-fashioned braid and hangs down her back, and the bright-green Mexican dress she is wearing as a nightgown is wrinkled from her sleep. She does not look any different since I last saw her, and we embrace warmly. I introduce her to Charles whom she has never met. She gets us the key, a long iron key, like a key to a city, and tells us how to find the house. We kiss again and say *à demain*.

La Mayonette is painted a rough yellow—the same yellow van Gogh used when he painted the houses there—and although there are several other buildings, mostly farm buildings, next to them, it looks garish and out of place. In the morning before I am properly awake, I can hear roosters crowing and a tractor starting up and setting off down the road. When I look around at the unfamiliar room—last night, not bothering to unpack, barely turning on a light, we all went straight to bed—I see an ordinary room sparsely furnished with a bedside table, two straight-backed chairs, and an armoire; only the wallpaper seems inappropriate. More than inappropriate: the wallpaper disturbs me. The design on it is a profile of a woman with red hair and dark sharp features, repeated a dizzying amount of times all around us. To make matters worse, the wallpaper was hung by an amateur. The faces do not match at the seams and are distorted—where there should be a nose, there is a chin, where there should be a mouth, hair.

In the next room, I can hear our two boys talking; their words are as distinct as if no wall separated us. "Shit," the younger boy says, "the bastard flew around me all night. I never got to sleep." He makes a buzzing sound and the older boy laughs. Something crashes to the floor and they both laugh. Already smiling, Charles opens his eyes and reaches an arm toward me. "We are going to have a good summer," he promises.

"In college, I read a story about a woman who goes crazy looking at the wallpaper in her bedroom," I answer.

La Mayonette is the name of the house we have rented in the Var district of France for the month of July. The house belongs to Francine's family and it was my idea to rent it, because of Francine, who was my classmate and friend a long time ago when I was a student in France, and because of the countryside. The countryside is hot and dusty and the azure sea and the crowded Riviera beaches, which are a few kilometers away and only a twenty-minute drive from the house, seem very remote from La Mayonette. Here the land is given over to vineyards and orchards and is contained by a ragged ring of scrub mountains on which grow patches of wild rosemary and thyme.

We are soon settled in La Mayonette and the days establish themselves into an easy routine. The two boys bicycle and run around as if they had always lived here and as if it does not matter that they are in France. The bread man delivers a loaf of flat round country bread every morning; and Jacqueline, who lives in one of the buildings clustered around La Mayonette, comes twice a week to clean and do the wash. She is silent and efficient and I am relieved that I do not have to speak to her and tell her what to do. Even so, I warn Charles to hide his money, his valuables; I do likewise. We learn our way around Pierrefeu, the little village perched on a hill six kilometers away. From there, we tour the *caves* to taste the wine grown in the region and end up buying two large plastic *bonbonnes* of pink and red wine—more than enough for a month, Charles says. We also buy a quantity of food: olive oil, tomatoes, garlic, fish, fruit—mainly the juicy yellow peaches that are in season.

On the Fourth of July, the younger boy says that he wants to bake a cake, but, inexplicably, he makes mashed potatoes instead. The kitchen is the largest room in the house and the one we use the most. A long oak table stands in the middle, and already, the tabletop is crowded with pitchers of wild flowers and china bowls of peaches. We have brought in two armchairs from the living room, and Francine is sitting in one of them and her two daughters, who are a little younger than our two boys, are sitting together in the other. The little French girls stare at our boys but do not speak to them, although I hope that by the end of the month they will. The two boys are mashing the potatoes with vigor and unaccustomed camaraderie, no doubt for the benefit of the little French girls.

Francine, her husband, Didier, and the two little girls stay for dinner. In addition to the mashed potatoes, we eat roast lamb and ratatouille. Afterward, Charles and Didier light firecrackers while the rest of us sit on the terrace and watch. I hold the younger boy by the arm to keep him out of the way and safe, but he manages to squirm out of my grasp. I don't much like fireworks—they make me afraid of burning flesh and dismemberment—but so as not to spoil the fun, I cheer with the others. "Bravo!" I shout. When the fireworks are done, we sit quietly and a little anticlimactically in the dark but star-filled Var night. The little girls have fallen asleep on Francine and Didier's laps and our two boys have disappeared inside the house, probably to read comic books. I look up at the sky for shooting stars—lovelier than fireworks.

La Mayonette, Francine explains to us, belonged to her aunt, her father's sister. When she was young, the aunt was very beautiful—Francine has seen photographs. She painted, she wrote poetry—Francine is not sure which but in any case the aunt was considered artistic. Mainly, the aunt kept to herself, Francine says, except that she loved dogs. When she died, there were more than a dozen dogs in the house—all kinds of dogs, strays for the most part—and, as a result, the people around here were afraid of her. Amongst themselves, they said she was crazy or else they said she was a witch—almost one and the same thing. Francine says she remembers coming over to La Mayonette as a child, for tea. Her aunt was fairly old by then, or, anyway, she seemed old to Francine; even so there was nothing about her to be afraid of. Her aunt had gotten quite stout and the dogs were friendly and benign. Poor woman, Francine says with a sigh, she was born with a third nipple—only Francine does not know the word for nipple in English, she uses the French word, *mamelon.* Of course, Francine adds, her aunt never married. No one speaks for a moment, then Francine says, "I worried a lot about it when my daughters were born, in case it is hereditary. One never knows, you know." She laughs a little and Didier makes a joke of it—something about more breasts to caress, he says, in French—and we all laugh.

Later, in bed, I confuse Francine's aunt with the woman in the wallpaper—no longer just a profile, the woman is depicted in her entirety and she is naked. Also, she is grotesque: on her body where there should be a leg, there is an arm, where there should be a hand, there is a foot. Charles touches me, and relieved, I wake up.

Every morning, Charles and I walk and our two boys bicycle down the drive of La Mayonette and across the main road to Francine's house. She has a swimming pool and a tennis court. Francine and I like to lie in the sun and watch while the children swim. In the water, they are friendlier, and the two boys are learning a bit of French. Francine and I talk: I talk in English, Francine answers me in French—this way it is easier for us both. Predictably, we talk about our children, our marriages, and what we do. Francine is a potter. We also reminisce about our student days and a trip we once took together to Egypt. We laugh when we talk about Egypt —what Francine remembers about the trip

I have completely forgotten and vice versa. I remember that on our last night, in Luxor, I slept with our tour guide and, afraid that Francine would disapprove, I did not tell her then—nor, although I am tempted to, do I tell her now. Francine sunbathes topless and, although unaccustomed, I do likewise. My breasts are not very big and when I lie flat on my back, one hardly notices them. Francine's breasts are bigger, and in spite of myself I think about her aunt.

Charles and Didier play tennis, and although Charles is tall and lanky and Didier is short and wiry, they seem evenly matched. One morning Charles wins, the next Didier wins. From the swimming pool, one can hear the ball bouncing and the two men keeping score. Since they keep score in French, to me it sounds as if they were playing another game, not tennis.

Charles disapproves of topless sunbathing on account of our two boys, he says, and on account of Didier, too, and when I hear that they have finished their game I put back the top of the bathing suit, and so does Francine. It has happened, however, that on one or two occasions I have pretended to fumble with the straps of my bathing suit. I have put back the top at the last minute so that when Charles and Didier walk from the tennis court to the swimming pool Didier can see me.

This morning while we were walking down the drive to go to Francine's pool, the younger boy, who was riding his bicycle ahead of us, was nearly hit by a car. The car that nearly hit him did not try to stop or to brake for him. At first, because the speeding car was between us and the boy, we imagined the worst had occurred and it was only when we ran across the road and saw that he was sitting cross-legged on the side of the road holding on to his arm, his bicycle on the ground next to him—the spokes of the front wheel bent, handlebars twisted wrong way around—that we realized that he was all right. Or almost all right.

On the way to the hospital in Toulon my husband drives and the younger boy sits on my lap. I stroke the back of his blond head at the same time that I try to protect him from the car's jolting motion. I also try not to look at his arm, which is already swollen and red and is dangling at such an odd angle that it looks as if it belonged on his other side. In the backseat, the older boy does not utter a sound, so that when we arrive at the hospital I have forgotten about him. "Oh, you are here, too," I say distractedly.

Only after we have been admitted to the emergency room and a nurse is cutting away his T-shirt with a pair of blunt-nosed scissors does the younger boy start to cry.

"Does it hurt a lot?" I ask him.

Sitting up on the examining table, the younger boy crosses his good arm protectively over his narrow, bare chest, he shakes his head no.

"Don't worry, we'll buy you a T-shirt just like it," I promise him lamely.

Nevertheless, while the doctor goes about setting his arm, I have to leave the room.

Back at La Mayonette, I suggest to the younger boy whose arm is now encased in shiny white plaster and held securely to his chest with a sling, that after all he has had to endure he should take a rest. He can lie down on my bed in our room for a while and I will read to him. But he refuses. He says he wants to go along with his brother to the swimming pool; even if he cannot swim, he can at least show the little French girls his cast, his sling. I don't insist. Instead, I tell Charles to go ahead with them if he wants to, but that I want to stay home.

It is around noon. Outside my bedroom window, I can hear the farmhands taking their midday break. Their lunch is spread out on the ground, as well as bottles of water and wine. The men are talking and laughing and I would have to concentrate to understand what they are saying, but I don't. I only listen to the sounds they make. Tomorrow is Bastille Day and I think that I can already hear the echoes of the holiday in their laughter. It is a laughter I cannot share and I envy their hard-earned, simple pleasures. From all four walls of the bedroom, dozens of sharp-faced, red-haired women are staring at me. "He is my boy," I say out loud and take off one of my sandals and hurl it as hard as I can at the woman nearest me in the wallpaper. I take off the other sandal and do the same thing, then I start to cry.

As a farewell dinner on our last night in Egypt, a *méchoui* was held, a few miles out in the desert. From Luxor, we were given the choice of getting there on horseback or on camelback. Most of the group, including Francine—she is frightened of horses—chose to go on camelback. I chose horseback, as did our tour guide. At the *méchoui,* there were Bedouins dressed in burnooses who roasted an entire sheep on a spit. There was a band playing indigenous music while a belly dancer with a sparkling stone pasted to her navel gyrated ceaselessly. A great deal of wine was served which we drank out of silver-looking cups. Afterward, on the way back to Luxor, the full moon was so bright that I could see the desert as clearly as if it were noon. The little Arab mare I was riding, unused, perhaps, to being out so late, was a bit nervous. Her gait, a half prance, half trot, rocked me pleasingly in the saddle. On his horse next to me, the tour guide rode so close that his knee pressed almost painfully into mine. This, too, added to my mare's excitement.

Although it is Bastille Day, we are subdued. The two boys are quiet. The younger one is tired—the cast, now decorated with drawings and signatures (even the cleaning woman, Jacqueline, has written her name on it) is bulky and uncomfortable—and he is also depressed. To try to cheer us up, Charles decides to drive to Ramatuelle for dinner. He takes the longer but more scenic road and, going around a sharp curve, we come perilously close to having a head-on collision with a van coming from the other direction; no one dares to say a word. In Ramatuelle, we walk single file down the picturesque narrow streets. On a whim, I announce that I want to go to the cemetery and visit the grave of Gérard Philipe, the actor. Our two boys have never heard of Gérard Philipe but they humor me as I tell them how Gérard Philipe died too young and at the height of his career and how the entire country mourned him. The cemetery overlooks the sea and is quite beautiful; even after all these years, there are a half a dozen bouquets of flowers heaped on top of Gérard Philipe's grave. Oddly, the cemetery makes me worry less about the younger boy's broken arm, and we enjoy our dinner in the restaurant. We stay and listen to the village band and watch the fireworks display. This time I am not frightened. It is late again when we drive home and in the car I hold Charles' free hand.

When I wake up the next morning I get out of bed and get dressed without waking Charles. I drive to Pierrefeu. Already, the streets there are crowded with housewives doing their morning shopping. To feel as if I belong with them, I buy milk and oranges; I also buy fresh croissants. A group of cyclists wearing yellow-and-black jerseys are getting ready for a race. They call out to each other: "Jean-Claude," "Jean-Pierre," "Jean-Marie"—all of them have double names—as they make their last-minute adjustments to their bikes. I stand and watch them for a while and one of the cyclists looks up and sees me watching him. I smile and tell him *bonne chance.* I am still smiling when the cyclist makes a braying noise at me—the high-pitched honking bray of a lonely donkey. He does it again so that the other cyclists with the double names look up from their bikes and laugh loudly. Startled and ashamed,

I quickly turn away. I realize that I have no business being there and that I have been gone much longer than I intended. Charles and our two boys must be awake by now and wondering where I am. I walk back to where I parked the car and drive home to La Mayonette as fast as I dare; as fast, no doubt, as the person who drove the car that nearly hit my son.

The last week of July is much hotter and we are not as energetic. We get up later and later each morning, and from our bed I count the woman's profiles. One hundred and seven—not including the profiles I cannot see, behind the armoire. Each time I get a different number, I start counting her profiles all over again. Also, Charles and I do not make love as often; when we do, my eyes are shut and I make believe that Charles is Didier. Afterward, I blame the red and pink wines we drank the night before; I blame the one hundred and seven profiles of the woman in the wallpaper watching—no, spying—on us; I blame myself. Outside, the air seems dense and hard to breathe; in the house, there are many more mosquitos and flies. The younger boy collects them in an empty jelly jar which he leaves on the table in the kitchen. I want to tell him not to, but I pick on him enough as it is. Also, he complains about how his arm in the cast itches and he does not sleep at night. Since he cannot swim, he spends most of the morning in the driveway under the pine trees where it is cooler, picking piñon nuts with the little French girls. Our boys tower over the little French girls, but at least they are speaking together. The two big *bonbonnes* of wine are nearly empty and neither Charles nor I can believe that we have drunk so much wine. "It does not seem possible," Charles says, shaking his head. Already, I am anxious at the prospect of leaving La Mayonette and I wonder when Francine and I will see each other again.

During our last meal together, after the four of us—Francine, Didier, Charles, and I—have finished off all the wine in the two large plastic *bonbonnes,* Didier brings out an old bottle of marc and we drink that. It is then—a little drunk—that I tell Francine that I went to bed with our tour guide in Egypt. "I only did it once," I tell her, and Francine laughs and says she had guessed it. She, too, sounds a little drunk—all four of us, probably, have drunk too much of the marc which is much stronger than the wine. And anyway, Francine continues, she slept with him as well. When I ask Francine how many times—once, twice, three times?—she only shakes her head so that the long braid down her back swings from side to side. Then I say to Didier who is sitting next to me, that now it is his turn to tell us something that he is ashamed of or that he regrets. Winking at me, Didier says: Nothing, nothing at all—*rien du tout.* In his entire life, Didier says again, there is nothing that he feels ashamed of or that he would not do over again if he had the chance, and Francine breaks in and says something sharp like: *"Tu te fous du monde, quoi!"* She sounds angry. To change the mood, Charles says that one of the things he feels most ashamed about happened a long time ago when he was a young boy, and it has nothing to do with sex. Quite the contrary, Charles says, it was while he was at boarding school and his mother used to write him a letter once a week and Charles never read those letters. In fact, Charles tells us, he never even bothered to open those letters, so that one time when he went home for the holidays and his mother unpacked for him she found all her letters there at the bottom of his suitcase, a whole packet of them, unopened.

The day we are to leave, Francine tells me that she thinks she is pregnant. "I haven't told anyone yet. Not even Didier, until I am sure. Naturally, this time, I hope it is a boy. But if it is another girl," she says, "I will name her after you."

Charles has packed the car and our boys' bicycles again are tied precariously upside down on the roof rack. I shake my head in disapproval. "This time, for sure, the bicycles are going to fall off,"

I tell Charles. Annoyed, he does not answer me. "We have so much more stuff than we came with," I complain. The older boy appears, carrying a large stack of French comic books—a parting gift, I suppose, from the little girls. "Can't you get rid of some of that?" I ask him. Exasperated, I go back inside La Mayonette for one last look and to see what we have forgotten. I find a hairbrush in the boys' bathroom, a few centimes on a bureau, one of Charles' ties hanging from the doorknob of our bedroom.

I would like to do something before we leave; I am not sure what. I stand irresolute in the middle of our bedroom. I hear Charles calling—they are waiting for me. Just before I walk out the door, I touch the wallpaper profile nearest me and I kiss the woman on the lips.

L'Esprit de L'Escalier

In the photograph, my mouth is slightly open. I am talking to the man sitting next to me. The man is the writer Alberto Moravia. Next to him, there is a woman. She is smiling at the camera, I can't think of her name. The fourth person in the photograph is Massimo. Massimo is looking off, looking away somewhere, looking elsewhere. This means that Massimo's face is seen in profile—you cannot see how good-looking he is. He is so good-looking, in fact, that Alberto Moravia said that he had made one of the characters in his book look just like Massimo, only this same character, Alberto Moravia said, had met a bad end.

Moravia gave me this book of his to read, but I left it in the car on the way home to Rome from Fregene. Fregene was where the photograph was taken. Fregene was where we had lunch the day I had to get into the car and drive back to Rome with Alberto Moravia instead of with Massimo.

His car, I remember, was custom built, special—something to do with the pedal you depressed to disengage the clutch. Alberto Moravia, you see, had a bad leg. He could not reach and push down on the clutch properly. The way Alberto Moravia drove was also, you might say, special. He drove very fast with one hand on my leg—high up on my leg.

When finally I arrived home, my father said he had been waiting for me. He wanted to know where I had been. "The beach," I said. "I was at the beach with Massimo." My father said, "No, no, Massimo has been killed."

I could hear my father snore every night that summer. Loud shuddering snores. Sometimes, the snores would wake him. Then my father would make another sound. A peevish sound. A sound of distress, also.

Most nights, I did not get home until three or four in the morning. One time, I did not get home until seven o'clock in the morning. It was light already and I could hear my father in the bathroom. The door to my room was shut and I just made it inside when the toilet flushed.

My boyfriend lived in Trastevere. I don't have a photograph of him but if I think of him, of us, I think of us eating spaghetti at a trattoria that stayed open all night that was right around the corner from where he lived. I remember I liked that part the best of everything, better than the making love—the eating spaghetti part. I liked sitting at the tables, the tablecloths stained with old tomato sauce, and I liked sitting next to him, our shoulders touching, and playing with the bread crumbs while we waited for the food to arrive. I liked sitting under the harsh unflattering late-night lights, the men who were there starting their day looking at me. Their look seemed to say that they knew we had just gotten through making love, which was the reason we were so hungry.

My father's office was on the fifth floor and the elevator was so old, to run it you still had to put a coin in it. The coin too, was hard to find, a ten-lire piece that nearly no longer existed. My father had to go all the way to a bank on the Piazza di Spagna to buy the ten-lire pieces he needed to use the elevator. But the elevator was how I met Massimo. Massimo was an architect and his office was right across the hall from my father's.

You could tell right away by the way Massimo said his *R*s that Massimo was not from Rome. Massimo was from the north, from Turin. Massimo knew a lot of people. He knew people like Silvana Mangano and like Lucia Bosé who married the bullfighter Dominguin, he knew Vittorio De Sica and Vittorio Gassman. Massimo even said he knew Anna Magnani. Massimo said he had had dinner with Anna Magnani once, and to prove it, Massimo said Anna Magnani spoke with her mouth full.

I don't remember how Massimo said he got to know Alberto Moravia or why Moravia asked Massimo to have lunch with him or, in turn, why Massimo asked me to go with him, but the one thing I do remember was how, in those days, Rome was like a small town. Everyone knew everyone and everyone knew what everyone was doing and whom he was sleeping with, and you always ran into someone somewhere—at one of the two or three good restaurants the tourists did not know about yet or at the outdoor nightclub off the Via Cassia where, at the very last possible moment, the stripper in the show turned out to be a man.

* * *

Massimo said that Moravia had also said not to forget to bring his bathing suit. The house, Moravia said, was next to the beach and Massimo, if he wanted to, could go swimming before lunch. In the car, on the way to Fregene, Massimo said he just remembered he had forgotten to bring his. But anyway, the day was hazy and overcast, he said. I told Massimo I would not go in the water alone, by myself. I would only go in if there was someone else. Or, if Massimo borrowed a bathing suit. I said to Massimo, too, then, that there was an undertow.

There was a lot of traffic that day and when Massimo and I arrived at Alberto Moravia's house we were late. Moravia said, "Hurry up, if you want to go in swimming. We're waiting for you to eat lunch." And Massimo—I'll never forget this—said, "No, no. I don't want to go in swimming, she does."

They watched me. I saw Alberto Moravia, Massimo, and the woman who was smiling in the photograph standing on the porch of the house holding bright red drinks watch me walk across the beach to the sea. A gray choppy sea, an end-of-the-summer sea, and I remember thinking: If I drown now it will be Massimo's fault. I also remember hearing Alberto Moravia say something about Americans—something about how only Americans would swim on a day like this. Americans, Moravia said, always had to prove things. But I did not look back at them. I put down my towel and I adjusted the straps on my bathing suit and I ran into the sea.

Massimo, as it turned out, also knew the woman who was smiling in the photograph. Massimo said she was a friend of his ex-wife, Ivy. Massimo had been married to Ivy for exactly four months. Instead of getting a divorce, he said, the marriage, thank God, had been annulled. Ivy was a model but Ivy, Massimo said, wanted to be an actress—she wanted to be discovered—and the only trouble with Ivy was that Ivy could only talk about shoes, about clothes. But he still saw her—Ivy. Massimo said he saw Ivy at those cafés on the Via Veneto, the Café de Paris and the other one across the street from it, the one next to the Hotel Excelsior. As a matter of fact, the last time he saw Ivy, Massimo said, was on the same day he had seen Vittorio Gassman and Massimo said he had told Ivy then how she had just missed him.

But to go back—back to the day Massimo's Lancia all of a sudden on the way back to Rome got a blowout and Massimo lost control of the car, the same day we had lunch with Alberto Moravia, the day I went in swimming, the day Alberto Moravia took the photograph with the camera he had showed us. The camera, Moravia said, had a special feature. If you set it, you would then have ten seconds to run back to your chair and to where you were sitting, which was exactly what Alberto Moravia did. He ran back with his bad leg and he bumped into the table and the wine glasses jiggled and some of my wine spilled.

But earlier and, as I was starting to say, when I came out of the water from swimming, everyone had left, everyone had gone back inside the house already. Alberto Moravia, Massimo, the woman who was smiling, all of them were sitting around the dining-room table eating as if they had forgotten about me completely. They were eating the antipasto and Moravia, without looking up at me, said, "Sit down, sit here," and I said to Massimo, "But I'm in my wet bathing suit still."

The woman who was smiling in the photograph stood up and took me into a bedroom—Alberto Moravia's bedroom. There, I took off my wet bathing suit and as I was standing with one foot in the air about to step into my underpants, the door opened and

Moravia walked in. Alberto Moravia said he just wanted to look for a book—his book, the same book he gave to me.

When I was dressed again and when I went back to the dining room, they were all twirling spaghetti on their forks—the second course. Moravia looked up at me and laughed. "You're a natural blond, after all," he said. I looked over at Massimo, but Massimo's face was bent over his plate. For a moment, I wasn't even sure I knew what Moravia was talking about and it was not until much later and until I was back in Rome that I thought of saying: No, you're wrong. I dye it blond.

There is a phrase for this, a French idiom exactly for when you only think of something to say afterward, after the event, for the apt phrase, for the perfect answer, but too late—*l'ésprit de l'éscalier.* As for what happened after lunch when Alberto Moravia told Massimo that Massimo should drive the woman who was smiling in the photograph back to Rome, and he, Alberto Moravia, would drive me in, and I wanted to say something—I wanted to object to this—this was not the same thing. For no matter how long or how hard I racked my brain for what to say to him—to this day even—I, for one, could never have come up with the right answer and I don't know if there is an expression for this.

In the car, with Moravia, I remember how, under my breath, I cursed Massimo. Massimo, I thought, should have stepped in. Massimo should have said something to Moravia like: No, I brought her here, and, you see, I know her father. Her father and I work on the same floor of the same office building. I promised to get her back safe and sound to him.

Also, on the way back to Rome from Fregene, I was thinking of how, the next time I saw him, I would not mince words with Massimo and of how, among other things, I would say to him: Not only was Alberto Moravia driving his custom-built car with the special clutch you depressed at a hundred miles an hour, and the whole time he had his hand on my leg, and I don't care how famous he is or that I can tell people later that I met him, I could have been killed. But also, I went in swimming, and it is a miracle that I did not drown and that I did not get pulled out to sea by the undertow, either.

Verdi

While Penny was staying on at the Donner Trail Ranch in Nevada—where she had gone to get a divorce—Penny's ex-husband, Mason, took his new wife, Sabrina, to Lourdes, France, on their honeymoon. Penny could never picture them there. Penny could not picture Mason standing in line to take the waters behind the sick—people who were carried there, people who arrived in wheelchairs, people who were covered with hideous running sores. Mason was too healthy, too sanguine, too big. As for Sabrina, Penny did not know what Sabrina looked like, but she pictured Sabrina pale, blond, with wrists the size of bird bones which Mason had to hold on to carefully.

The ranch was in the foothills of the Sierra Nevadas in a place called Verdi, named after the composer—only the name was pronounced Ver*die*, as Penny did eventually, despite her sense of how things ought to be. Had Giuseppe Verdi actually come over to

America? Penny had asked a ranch hand named Mike on her first day—this was the sort of thing Mason would have known. And was this where Giuseppe Verdi—Penny was still pronouncing the name right, only she had the composer wrong—got the idea for what was it called, *La fanciulla del West*? Mike said no, he did not know; Mike said he had forgotten most of his Spanish, anyway. Mike was busy tightening the cinch on the saddle of the horse she was going to ride that day. A horse named Thunderbolt. Penny was about to say something more about Giuseppe Verdi, instead she said: Is he gentle? I haven't been on a horse in years.

To her surprise, Penny liked Verdi. She liked the Donner Trail Ranch, she liked the horseback riding, the people who, like her, were waiting to get their divorces; Penny even said she liked the look of the tumbleweed on the road. Also, Penny liked Mike, and after the requisite six weeks were up, after all the papers were signed and sealed, even after she had thrown her gold wedding band into the Truckee River, Penny—it was June—was still lounging around the ranch pool with Inge.

Penny and Inge had got into the habit of driving to Reno together to do their wash. After loading the machines with their dirty clothes, they would run across the street from the laundromat to Harrah's Casino. Penny liked to play the slot machines while Inge sat at a table and played baccarat or chemin de fer. Usually Inge would lose and Penny would win, usually, too, Penny would end up treating Inge to the dimes she needed to dry her jeans.

Inge was Danish, she spoke with a slight accent; Inge had been in one film. She told Penny how she took pills to stay thin, pills to get brown, pills to make her sleep. Inge also told Penny that she had been married three times—twice to the same man whom she was divorcing again, and once to the film maker. Penny told Inge about Mike.

Yes, Mike with his battered hat worn at an angle was handsome; yes, Mike with his long booted legs could stick to a horse like a burr; but had Mike finished high school? Penny wondered. The subject never came up. At night, after she finished her dinner, Penny went to meet Mike in the only bar in Verdi—a roadhouse situated on the highway. Penny would walk there from the Donner Trail Ranch, the headlights from the big semis heading west toward the Bay Area lighting up her way.

Penny and Mike drank Coors and played pool—that was how it started—Mike leaning into her teaching her how to hold the cue stick. Also, Mike telling Penny how, at home in Wyoming, he and his girlfriend used to play not for money, not for beers, but for going down on each other—the loser had to. Penny did not know what to answer. I bet I've grossed you out, Mike guessed, watching her. Penny laughed, denied it.

In the mornings while it was still cool, Penny and—the number varied—two or three people from the ranch, usually—usually, Inge never got out of bed before noon—went horseback riding. Either Mike or Ron, the other ranch hand, who claimed that he had broken every bone in his body at least once bronco-busting, would take them up the mountains. Thunderbolt was part quarter horse and after Penny got used to how fast he could turn—the first time Thunderbolt went through a gate, Penny found herself nearly on the ground clinging to the pommel—she always asked for him. Thunderbolt had a soft mouth, changed leads easily, did not spook or get winded. Suddenly, all the horse-talk Penny had not talked since she was a young girl or married to Mason came back to her—hocks, withers, snaffle, and curb bits—and, on an impulse on one of the trips to Reno with Inge, Penny bought herself a pair of leather chaps just like the ones Mike always wore.

In the clothing store, Inge had tried on a pair of green lizard cowboy boots that cost four hundred and fifty dollars. Hand-stitched, and anywhere else, those boots, the salesman told Inge, would cost her double, while Inge who was walking up and down the length of the store admiring her feet said she was feeling lucky that day. Inge also told Penny that anyway, during the night when she could not sleep, she had had second thoughts—Denmark was boring. She was going back to Los Angeles, her second husband, the film maker owned a big house, and Penny had said: Oh, no, you'll marry *him* again!

One of the things Penny told Mike she wanted to do while she was staying at the ranch was ride the Donner Trail—at least, the part where the party had started to cross the Sierra Nevadas and was surprised by an early snowstorm. And although Penny had read about it in school years ago, she could, to this day, she said, remember all the gory details: how many of the party had died, and, of course, how the others had survived.

Mike said he would take Penny on his day off, only it was too far for them to ride horseback. The Donner Pass was in California—not in Nevada, and the Donner Trail Ranch was just a name—and Mike would take Penny there in his truck. They would make a day of it, go on to Grass Valley or to dinner in Sacramento. They could spend the night somewhere, Mike also said, in a big king-size bed with real cotton sheets for a change, and Penny told Mike that Inge was the only person who knew, the only person she had told anything to.

How many times already had she walked down the highway and met Mike at the roadhouse, drunk a few beers, then gone back with him to make love? Mike was younger than she was, Mike had never had children, and what Mike said for him had started as no big deal—Penny's cute ass on top of Thunderbolt was what he said he had noticed first—was different now, and the funny part, Mike also said, was that he really loved Penny and he did not want her to leave. In the distance, beyond the highway, Penny could hear dogs barking but Mike said they sounded more like coyotes to him; Mike had his arm around her and he squeezed Penny tighter to him.

At the Nevada state line, the inspection station official made Mike stop the truck. He made Mike and Penny step out of the truck on to the highway while he looked inside. He asked Mike if he was carrying any fruit, any plants.

"The bastard," Mike said when he drove on again.

"What were they really looking for? Drugs?" Although the day was warm, Penny shivered. Who would explain if she was killed in a car crash with Mike? What would, for instance, Inge tell Mason?

A little over one hundred years ago, Penny began, to change the subject, the eighty-nine people who were to make up the Donner Party left Springfield, Illinois, for California, and Penny said she could almost see the twenty covered wagons drawn by oxen filled with provisions—beans, potatoes, squash, eggs packed in cornmeal, rice, tea, coffee—and the milk cows—funny too what had stayed in her head: to make butter, all the women needed to do was put the cream in the churn and let the jolting wagons do the rest.

"Are you listening?" Penny interrupted herself.

"Yeah, butter. Go on." Mike put one hand inside Penny's leg.

"No, not now," Penny said.

Crossing the plains, Penny continued, the men were able to fish, shoot game. After killing a buffalo, often they would just slit the animal's throat and extract the tongue, leaving the rest of the buffalo meat. At night, after supper, they played games, danced, sang; occasionally there was an accident—Penny was warming up to her story—the time a pony fell and crushed a young boy's leg and they nearly had to amputate. Another time, a knife fight broke out between two men and resulted in the death of one of them. There was the danger of Indian attacks—luckily, the Paiute

Indians had a reputation for being lazy. Another potential danger, Penny said, was bears; but the bears were about to go into hibernation which meant that they were full and sleepy. Everyone knew that the worst time to meet a bear was in the—

"Hell, you are making all this up," Mike said.

"No, no, it's true. I read it somewhere."

"You read it where? Not everything you read in books is true, you know."

"Well, I might be wrong about the bears hibernating, but the rest of it is true. I know," Penny said.

"I nearly ran into a bear once," Mike said. "Come to think of it, it was in November, and this bear cannot have been sleepy, but he sure must have been full."

"Where?" Penny said.

"In Wyoming. I was out looking for some calves that were missing. I found them all right," Mike continued. "A bear had gotten two of them—you should have seen them, it was like he had split them right down the middle and it couldn't have been more than an hour or two since he had done it either, their innards were lying exposed on the ground, all torn up, half-eaten. It was pitiful. I couldn't get my horse closer than fifty yards of them. The smell of bear was too fresh, I guess. Too strong."

"Oh," Penny said.

Due to unforeseen difficulties crossing the Humboldt Sink, after a pause Penny had resumed, the Donner Party did not reach the Sierra Nevadas until mid-October. Already, there was snow on the ground. Food was getting scarce, the oxen could not get enough grass to eat and were getting weak. Twice the Donner Party tried to cross the pass, twice the deep snow drove them back. By November, Penny told Mike, the Donner Party's food had run out completely—they had eaten everything including their pet dogs.

At Truckee, Mike and Penny turned off the highway; the site where the Donner Party had spent their horrific winter was off route 40; across the way, there was a convenience store. Mike said he wanted to go and buy a few beers. He also wanted to buy some cold cuts, he said, some bread, some cheese. He and Penny could have a picnic.

"Did you know that nearly half of the Donner Party died?" Penny said when Mike caught up with her. She was standing in front of a big rock with a plaque on it. The plaque listed all the names of the members of the Donner Party. "Only forty-seven out of the eighty-nine people survived."

Mike held out a bag of groceries, a blanket he had taken from the back of his truck.

"We can sit on this," he said.

"Hard to imagine, isn't it? But you never know to what lengths people will go if they are starving to death, do you?" Penny said.

Mike said, "That's right. I got bread, salami, two kinds of cheese. They were out of Coors so I got a six-pack of Millers."

Penny said, "I can't imagine—where would you even begin? With an arm? A leg?"

Mike said, "I left the truck in the parking lot. There is nothing in it to steal—nothing but the truck itself, I guess."

Penny laughed. "Who would want to steal your old truck?" Then she said, "That reminds me of a story my husband, Mason—no, I mean my ex-husband, Mason—told me about this farmer in France."

Mike said, "France? I've been to Canada."

"The story is about this French farmer during the war and each week the French farmer rides his bicycle past the same German officer and the farmer is carrying this big sack. And every week, the German officer stops the farmer and makes him get off his bicycle while he inspects the sack. The sack is filled with potatoes, turnips, cabbages—whatever—and of course the German officer is convinced that the French farmer is smuggling something. Each week, the German officer does the same thing: he makes the French farmer get off the bicycle and he goes through the sack to make sure. This goes on during the entire war, and no matter how hard he looks, the German officer never finds anything in the French farmer's sack."

"I bet I've heard this story before," Mike said, handing Penny a beer he had opened.

"Wait. Let me finish." Penny took a sip of the beer. "The war ends and just before the German officer goes back to Germany, he sees the French farmer one more time and he says to him: Listen, this business with you every week with that big sack is not going to let me sleep nights. Now that the war is over and it no longer matters, do me a favor and tell me what it was you were smuggling. And you know what the French farmer answers?" Penny asks Mike.

"Bicycles."

Sitting with his long legs crossed on the blanket next to the rock with the plaque on it, Mike was cutting up the salami. He handed Penny a slice on the point of his pocketknife and Penny shook her head. She said she was not that hungry and anyway, she had decided all of a sudden to become a vegetarian. Mike laughed and said that Penny had to eat to keep up her strength, and Mike also said he was not kidding around as he waved the slice of salami on the point of his knife closer to Penny's mouth. Again Penny shook her head, she made the neighing sound of a horse balking at crossing a bridge or balking at something and Mike took both her arms in his free hand and held them together so hard that Penny had to open her mouth and let Mike force-feed her the salami slice. When he let go of her arms, she was planning to spit the salami out, but Mike had second-guessed her. Still holding on to Penny's arms, he said to her: First, chew it down good.

In the motel that night, Penny said she had a headache. The room had two beds in it and Penny and Mike each slept in one of them. Penny pulled up the covers over her head while Mike watched television. She could hear the voices on a talk show, and she could see the glow of the set through the synthetic material of the bedspread. Also, she could hear the sound of the trucks on the highway. The motel was situated at the bottom of a hill and all the trucks changed into a lower gear right outside the window.

The snow at Donner Lake had reached twenty-two feet. Penny had seen the marker. She had also overheard someone there say that twenty-two feet was nothing compared to the winter of '52. Then it had snowed sixty-nine feet and the pass was closed for twenty-eight days. Four hundred people were trapped inside a train, food had to be brought to them on snowshoes; also a doctor.

When Penny got back to the Donner Trail Ranch, she told Inge that the night in the motel was the first time since she had been in Verdi that the divorce seemed real to her, the first time too—even if Mike was snoring away in the bed next to hers, although Penny did not tell Inge this—that she had felt alone. Really alone. And being alone, Penny went on to tell Inge, was not necessarily such a bad thing either, it was different that's all. Inge told Penny yes, and to just please take a look at her. Inge was wearing the green lizard cowboy boots. Penny was not going to believe this but for the first time since *she* had been in Verdi, Inge had been lucky and won a lot of money at chemin de fer.

The next time Penny went riding on Thunderbolt, Ron—not Mike—took her and the others out. Penny only got to see Mike later when she returned from the ride. Mike was outside the barn shoeing a big bay horse. The horse was the horse Mike usually rode. The horse's two front legs were hobbled, and Mike, with his back up against the horse's rear, had one of the horse's back legs firmly wedged in between his own legs. Mike was cleaning around the horse's frog with a hoof pick, and the big bay horse was nervously whisking his black tail back and forth in Mike's face. Without looking up from what he was doing, Mike was telling the horse to, damnit, quit that. Penny stood with her hands on her hips watching Mike.

"You know the story you told me?" Mike said, straightening up and putting the bay horse's hoof down and not looking at Penny. "I heard the exact same story before, only instead of a French guy it was a Mexican, an old Mexican with a sack crossing the border into Texas, and the punch line, too, was different. It was *horses.*"

In the end, Penny had spat out the salami. She had chewed and chewed and chewed but still she could not make the meat go down. Her throat had closed to it, she had gagged. Also, she knew how she must look—her jaws working away uselessly, her eyes filling up with tears. Okay, you don't have to eat it, was what Mike had finally said to her.

Fortitude

The naked woman in the floor show at the nightclub on Pat Pong Road is blowing smoke rings from down there—perfect round smoke rings. Each time she puts the cigarette to her lips, the guys in the audience start to whistle and catcall and stamp their feet. The noise they make is so loud, so deafening, I can't hear myself speak—not that I want to speak particularly.

Just think of it, my husband says to me when the show is over and the lights have come back on and he has ordered us two more beers. Think of the muscles she must have down there.

Poor woman, I say. In spite of myself I light up a cigarette. Look. I show him. I can't even blow an ordinary smoke ring. And I've smoked for how long? Since I was fifteen? Jesus, I also say, shaking my head.

Yeah, which reminds me, my husband says, drinking his beer.

In a club in Vientiane, I saw a woman put a ping-pong ball inside her. She made the ping-pong ball bounce up and down on the floor and all the guys watching her tried to grab the ping-pong ball as a souvenir. My husband puts his hand in his pants pocket then takes it out again, his hand closed, holding something. See, he says to me, opening his hand quickly.

Don't, I say.

Yesterday, when I arrived from the States at Don Muang Airport, I did not right away recognize my husband. From where I was standing waiting to go through customs, I mistook him for another man. I waved and smiled excitedly to this other man. Fortunately my husband was standing not far from this other man and he waved and smiled back at me and I did not have to explain that after the eighteen-hour flight I was tired probably and not seeing things right. Also, my husband has lost weight. His blond hair, too, is cropped short, and when I first put my hand through it, his hair felt prickly and strange.

The other thing I noticed about the woman in the floor show is that she has shaved off her pubic hair. But then again, orientals, I've heard, don't have much body hair. This goes for the men as well. Most oriental men don't bother to shave. They pluck the hair out with tweezers or else they leave a little tuft of the hair growing—like those long hairs that grow out of a mole—for good luck or good karma.

I don't know, my husband continues, oriental women don't really do it for me. They're too little or something. He leans over and squeezes my knee with one hand.

Lucky for me, I say, moving my leg away.

The woman who was in the floor show is sitting at the bar now. She is drinking a diet Coke and she is dressed again in a flower-print dress. I watch as a fellow, a fellow in uniform, goes up to her and offers her a cigarette. A Marlboro cigarette. The woman shakes her head.

I nudge my husband and point my chin toward the woman. You know what? I tell him. She doesn't smoke.

In bed in the hotel, I cannot sleep. Despite the ceiling fan which makes the noise of a jet plane taking off, the room is too hot. Also, my time, it is only ten o'clock in the morning yesterday; and I drank too much beer. Each time I shut my eyes everything in the hotel room spins and I start feeling sick to my stomach. Jim, my husband, is snoring lightly. Occasionally, he jerks an arm up in the air and mutters something. I think of the other man at the airport I mistook him for. Once I got closer, I saw that the other man had bad acne scars and did not look a bit like my husband. The thought that I could make such a mistake embarrasses me. More than embarrassment, I feel ashamed. So much so that, earlier, while we were making love, I had half hoped that my husband, in the heat of his passion, would call out a name. Not my name, an oriental woman's name. The oriental woman's name which inexplicably comes to my mind is Madame Chiang Kai-shek.

Early the next morning on the way to the beach, Jim and I sit in the backseat of a jeep. The man who is driving the jeep is called Maynard, the man sitting next to him wears glasses and is called Evan. Maynard and Evan are in the same company as my husband, Alpha Company; all three men are on R&R in Thailand for a week. The traffic getting out of the city is heavy. We stop, start, honk, start again.

With a groan, Jim puts his head on my shoulder. I've a helluva hangover, he says.

Evan turns in his seat and asks me, So how do you like Bangkok? Have you been out here before?

I shake my head no. We went to Wat Prah Keo, yesterday, I offer. Pretty amazing. All that gold.

Yeah? I've never been. Evan turns back. He says something to Maynard that I cannot hear and that makes Maynard laugh.

Wise ass, my husband calls out to them.

Bitch, Maynard swears at a samlor driver who cuts in front of the jeep. Fuckingcuntbitch. Then remembering me, he says, *Pardon*—pardon with a French accent.

I've never been to the Far East before. The farthest east I have ever been—only to me, then, it was west—was Hawaii last year on our honeymoon. Also, I have not seen my husband in eight months and since he has been sent overseas.

My husband's arm is around my shoulder, with his other hand he is picking at and feeling the material of my blouse.

Nice. New? he asks.

I bought it at that dress shop next to the gourmet deli on—I start to tell him when, with the same hand, he starts fondling my breast. Stop, I also tell him, gesturing toward the two men sitting in the front of the jeep.

My husband shrugs. He puts his head on my shoulder again and shuts his eyes. He sleeps or feigns sleep.

The road to Pattaya is paved but narrow and full of potholes which Maynard tries to avoid. To do this, Maynard sometimes drives the jeep on the wrong side of the road; sometimes, too, he only gets back on the right side of the road at the last possible moment when another car or truck is bearing down on us from the other direction. I make myself look away, or I look out the side window at the paddy fields. The paddy fields are so green they nearly look yellow; an occasional palm tree marks the blurry horizon. Along the road, children are selling sugarcane. To try to stop us, the children wave the sugarcane at the jeep. Once, when a sugarcane stalk raps against the side of the jeep, instinctively, I draw back.

In the front seat, Evan is flipping through a guidebook. He is practicing his Thai out loud.

Nung, sorng, sarm, see, har, hok, jeht.

Can you quit that? Maynard tells him.

Then, all of a sudden, without warning it begins to rain. First one big drop of rain at a time falling on the windshield, then faster and faster the rain comes pelting down. We pass a woman on a bicycle and I see her swerve on the bicycle, but on account of the rain I don't see whether or not she falls off the bicycle. I can no longer make out the road or the rice paddies out the window.

Damn, Maynard says. I can't see a damn thing.

Christ, Jim says, sitting up. The noise of the rain has woken him up. What the hell was that?

Rain, I say.

Jim looks at me for a minute as if he doesn't know who I am. What? he asks, frowning.

It's raining, I say again.

His face clears. Shit. I guess I was dreaming, he answers.

Sip, sip-eht, sip-sorng, sip-sarm, sip-see, Evan continues.

Evan, I can't drive if you don't shut the fuck up! Maynard shouts at him.

Pattaya is not how I imagined it—I imagined a long stretch of deserted white sand with lush palm fronds and red and purple bougainvillea branches lining the shore. Instead, the shore front is filled with ugly cement buildings, restaurants, fast food stands. Everywhere misspelled signs in English advertise clubs, massage parlors, boats for hire. In our small and sparsely furnished one-room bungalow, Jim is lying on his back on the bed, his hands are clasped behind his head. A slight sea breeze stirs the curtains in the window. Next door a radio is playing, a man sings like Chubby

Checker: *Lock to the light, lock to the left.* Jim is watching me unpack, then he watches me undress.

Don't you want to go swimming? I am naked and standing awkwardly with one foot inside my bathing suit.

I think I'll take a nap, Jim answers. I'm beat.

I'll just go for a quick dip, I tell him.

Yeah, and watch out for sharks! Jim calls out after me.

The beach is crowded with Thai families and their children, thin-legged boys hawking cold drinks and hot spicy food on sticks, soldiers on leave drinking beer. A few of the soldiers have Thai women with them; one soldier has a small brown bear on a leash sitting next to him. The brown bear looks hot, sick. I walk past a bunch of soldiers who are playing a noisy game of volleyball. One of them holds out the volleyball to me, I shake my head and keep walking. Finally I set my towel and bag with suntan lotion and a book in it down on the sand. I don't see Maynard or Evan anywhere.

The ocean is warm and the water is very shallow. I have to walk quite a way out before the water reaches my waist and before I can swim. I am a good swimmer but instead of swimming my usual crawl, I keep my head out of the water, I keep an eye out for sharks. Also, for water-skiers. The speedboats pulling them along race back and forth heedlessly and too close to the shore.

The summer I was fourteen, my family went to stay with my mother's sister in her cabin on a lake in northern Maine and there I developed a crush on my first cousin, Carl. Carl was a little older and he was a natural-born athlete as well as an avid water-skier. From the back of a speeding motorboat I used to watch him do stunts like turn completely around on his skis and not fall in. Also I remember how Carl offered to teach me how to water-ski, but for some reason that I no longer remember—maybe I had my period and I was embarrassed—I declined. A few years later, Carl lost his arm in a freak traffic accident, but Carl's fortitude was so exemplary, his mother, my aunt, said, that undeterred, he continued to sail, to play golf, to play tennis, to do everything exactly the way he had before. I saw Carl again not too long ago at his wedding; I even danced with him—a good dancer and never missing a step, Carl held me tightly with his one arm—and I told him how I regretted not taking him up on his invitation to teach me how to water-ski. Waterskiing was easy and the least of it, Carl answered me; on account of the music and all the people talking around us, he must have misunderstood me, for he went on to tell me how he still could feel sensation in his missing arm. A phantom limb, he called it.

When I go back to my towel on the beach, the bag with the suntan lotion and my book in it is gone. When I go back to the one-room bungalow, Jim is lying exactly how I left him, he is asleep on the bed.

What was the book? Maynard asks me at dinner.

The four of us are seated at a table at an outdoor restaurant. The restaurant has a Thai name and the sign for it at the entrance shows a picture of rock lobsters boiling inside a pot. When Jim orders a rock lobster, the waiter shakes his head.

Mai mi—not here—he says.

But the sign, Jim points and starts to argue with him.

Leave it, Evan tells him. The sign means shit.

The Bell Jar, I answer, by Sylvia Plath, she was a poet.

Oh, yeah, I've heard of her. She killed herself.

How? Jim asks.

She gassed herself in the oven while her children were asleep.

What's a bell jar? Evan asks.

It's a glass jar you put over small plants, seedlings really—I start to say, when suddenly a coconut falls out of a tree and on top of our table. The coconut smashes dishes and scatters the cutlery; it breaks a glass and a bottle full of beer rolls into my lap.

Jim! I yell.

In his hurry, Jim has knocked over his chair.

Jim, I say again.

Sorry, Jim says. He is embarrassed; also he has gone very white. I overreacted, he says.

Maynard picks up Jim's chair, then pats Jim on the back. No big deal, man. Sit down. It can happen to any of us.

Neither Evan nor Maynard look over at me.

Look, I say to change the subject. I point to a sign tacked up to a nearby tree: *People having fragrant names do not liter here.* What do you suppose that means?

When we come back from the restaurant and before we go to bed, Jim and I sit on the wooden steps leading up to our one-room bungalow. We look up at the stars and smoke cigarettes. Jim has his arm around me.

That writer, Sylvia what's-her-name, why did she kill herself? he asks me.

I don't know. She was depressed, I guess. Depressed about her writing, I answer.

Jim—

What?

Nothing. I wonder who stole my book, I say instead. Some kid, probably.

Jim squeezes my shoulder and we stand up and go inside.

In bed, I get on top but Jim says he is too tired to make love now. Still, I try to arouse him; I kiss his chest, I kiss his nipples; he pushes away my head.

The other thing I remember about our stay at my mother's sister's cabin on a lake in northern Maine was how, upstairs, from my bedroom window I looked directly down on the outdoor shower. Without even wanting to, I could see how my mother and my aunt soaped in between their legs, I could see how tenderly my aunt washed her large breasts, how carefully my father pulled back the foreskin to wash his penis, and how, wet, the black hairs on my uncle's back and buttocks formed themselves into perfect ringlets. One time I watched Carl start to masturbate but the awful grimace on his upturned face made me turn away from the window—the same awful grimace that was on his face, maybe, when the arm that was sticking out of his car window got shattered by a pickup truck whose driver ran the stop sign at an intersection.

The next morning, the four of us go to the beach. Evan brings along a deck of cards and we sit on our towels facing each other, we take turns playing gin rummy.

You should watch your back, Maynard tells me.

I turn to look around.

No, I mean the sun, he says. You'll get toasted.

You're right, I say. Already, my back feels stiff, sore.

Gin! Evan says again and again as he slaps another card facedown. He keeps winning and after a while I stand up and tell Jim I am going in for a swim.

I'll go with you.

With Jim next to me in the water, I feel safer. I don't worry so much about sharks or motorboats. When we have swum so far out that I can no longer make out Evan and Maynard sitting on the beach, I turn over on my back. Jim does likewise. We float for a while without speaking, letting the little warm waves lap at us, jog us a little. For the first time, since I have been in Thailand visiting Jim, I feel good and like my own self again.

You know, I like your hair short, I say turning back on to my stomach and paddling toward Jim. It feels nice, kind of like bristles.

Yeah? Jim holds me by the shoulders. What kind of bristles? He butts me lightly with the top of his head. We are both treading water. He butts me again a little harder.

Badger bristles?

Already Jim is pulling down the straps of my bathing suit. Take it off, he tells me.

Here?

Yeah, here.

Because making love in the ocean is awkward, I start to laugh. When I laugh, I swallow water. The sea water makes me cough. The more I cough the more water I swallow.

I'm going to drown, I say, in between coughing and spitting out seawater. Jim, I mean it, I also say. With one hand I cling to Jim, with the other I cling to my bathing suit; our heads, like loosened buoys, bob up and down in the ocean.

Jesus, Jim finally says.

When we get back to the beach, Maynard has left and Evan is sitting cross-legged on the towel smoking a joint. He holds out the joint toward Jim and, closing his eyes, Jim takes a long drag from it. Then, he passes the joint on to me. Not to appear unfriendly or prudish, I take a small puff and hand the joint back to Evan. During our absence, the beach has gotten crowded again. Next to us, her long dark hair framing and fanning her face, a young Thai woman in a bikini is squatting astride a man, massaging his large pink back.

It is dark when we drive back to Bangkok. From time to time, the headlights from oncoming cars and trucks illumine the inside of the jeep. Some cars do not dim their headlights and momentarily blind us; the other headlights, on account perhaps of the potholes, bounce weirdly around and briefly illumine the deserted paddy fields that border the road. Maynard who is driving again asks, How much longer are you staying over here?

Another four days, I answer. In the backseat, I squeeze Jim's hand.

What are you guys going to do? Evan turns around just as a passing car lights up his exaggerated wink.

What's it to you, Jim answers him. Maybe we'll head up to Chiang Mai. Chiang Mai is a lot cooler.

Sounds good to me, I say, giving Jim's hand another squeeze.

No one says anything for a while, then, all of a sudden, Evan says, Hey! I'm thinking of someone.

Who? Ho Chi Minh!

Westmoreland, the asshole!

Is it a woman? I ask.

Yes, Evan answers.

Is she alive?

No.

Madame Nhu?

Was she good looking? Maynard also says.

Marilyn Monroe, Mae West, Eva Braun, Janis Joplin, Amelia Earhart—excited, Jim nearly shouts.

Right. I laugh. Typhoid Mary, I say next. Although I am pretty sure I know who the woman Evan is thinking of is, I don't want to say her name yet. I want to go on guessing and playing the game. Bloody—I start to say when the inside of the jeep is again illumined. This time the light is brighter and does not move past us. I see Evan put his hand up to his face and I turn to say something to Jim when we hit.

Jim moves underneath me on the floor and for a crazy moment I think we are making love. Then he hits me hard on the chin with his elbow as he tries to get up. I have been thrown on top of him.

Are you okay?

I don't know. I guess, I say.

Jesus! Jim says. We've hit a truck. A goddamn truck.

Jim climbs over me and pulls at the door on Maynard's side. Maynard! I hear him yell. Maynard, come on. Help me get this damn door open! Evan! Hey, man! he also yells.

Maynard is slumped over the wheel and the horn is blaring. Next to him, I see only part of Evan's back.

Jim! I say.

In the front seat, Maynard finally sits up and the horn stops blaring. Shit, he says. What happened? Oh, God, Evan? Evan! he also yells.

In the backseat, I am holding my shoulder up with one hand. My shoulder does not hurt, but I cannot feel it.

Maynard gets his door open and nearly falls out of the jeep. There is blood on his pants. Jim is already standing in the middle of the road. He is shouting, Get help! Get an ambulance for chrissakes!

A yellow bus has stopped right alongside of us. People are looking down curiously from the bus windows. Someone is speaking in Thai, speaking in a fast singsong, the words sound like nonsense. I pull myself out of the jeep. I am still holding up my shoulder and I have started to feel it. I feel it a lot.

Is Evan okay? I ask stupidly.

Evan's cheek is resting on top of the smashed hood of the jeep, shards from the windshield twinkle in his hair and on his face. His glasses which miraculously are not broken, dangle down still hooked around his ear. His eyes and mouth are open and dark blood is streaming from his nose.

The road is lit now with the uneven wavering of headlights; people have stopped and gotten out of their vehicles to look at the accident. They have formed a semicircle around the jeep and stare at us from a polite distance; out of embarrassment, they are grinning.

The truck driver stands next to Maynard. He has a red bandana wrapped pirate-style around his face and he pantomimes holding and turning a make-believe steering wheel. The hood of his truck is smashed in as well, a headlight is swinging from a wire; a good-luck jasmine *pon* hangs limply from the truck's fender. An agitated honking noise is coming from the back. Geese. He is transporting a load of geese.

Gold Leaf

In the village of Rossinière, in Switzerland, Amy is handed a piece of gold leaf to eat.

"It's good for the digestion," Cécile tells her in her accented English. "It's good against arthritis, too."

Both girls laugh. Both girls are too young to worry yet about arthritis.

"I eat it all the time—an expensive habit. My parents would be furious if they knew," Cécile says, as she goes back to the lamp which she is restoring and to which she is applying the gold. Her strokes are quick and sure and she uses a curious instrument with an agate head to make the gold shine.

Amy shuts her eyes and puts the gold leaf—a little gelatinous and more like mercury than gold—into her mouth. The gold feels like paper and, because her mouth has gone dry, she has difficulty swallowing it. With an effort, she forces the gold down and feels its uneasy passage down her throat. The gold has no taste.

This is Amy's first time in Switzerland and her first week in Rossinière where she is living with Cécile and her family for the summer. Cécile's family owns an antique store that specializes in Swiss hand-painted furniture which they restore and sell. The painted furniture reminds Amy of American Quaker or Pennsylvania Dutch furniture, only it is more artful, more intricate. The armoires and chests in the Cottiers' store as well as in their house have elaborately painted scenes, landscapes with churches, castles, people, carriages, animals. The colors, too, are a surprise: bright mountain greens, vivid sky blues, startling blood reds, nothing like the more sober and muted Quaker and Pennsylvania Dutch colors. Amy's bed in the Cottiers' house, for instance, is decorated with lush garlands of blue and red flowers which inspire her with an unaccustomed gaiety. Already, Amy claims that she sleeps better here than she does elsewhere.

"Funny," Amy has told Cécile and her parents, "I had expected Swiss art to be, you know, kind of dour and sad. Instead, it's very lively, it's very—" Unable to think of the proper word, Amy blushed, stopped.

In addition, Amy likes the Swiss furniture because each hinge, each fastening and joint, however old, still works simply and perfectly, and Amy says that, for the time being anyway, she prefers craftsmanship to invention. Also, she says she likes the fact that all the furniture is clearly dated. *Josef et Marie-Thérèse Henchot—1785* is painted below the garland of blue and red flowers on the headboard of Amy's bed so that she does not need to speculate or guess, or, in turn, be wrong.

Cordial and noncommittal with Amy, Cécile's parents, Monsieur and Madame Cottier, right away include her in their routine with neither surprise nor, as far as Amy can see, any adjustments. Their lack of curiosity about her and her family, Amy attributes to discretion rather than to indifference; when Amy on the first evening volunteered that she was a twin, Madame Cottier did not immediately ask Amy if her twin was identical or fraternal the way everyone else always did.

Instead the conversation around the Cottiers' dining room table tends to remain general and devoid of those personal remarks and innuendos Amy resents in her own family (although one time, Madame Cottier did mention Cécile's short—no, shorn—hair, and with a look of long suffering on her face said to Amy: "You should have seen her hair before! Beautiful thick hair! Now, she looks like—how can I say?—one of those poor people, one of those victims!")

Mostly, however, the talk is about food. Monsieur and Madame Cottier discuss the quality of the *gruyère* and whether it has aged properly, the butter and whether such-and-such a dairy is better than another or whether it has fallen off in quality, they speak about the peaches and whether they are as good, as ripe, as firm, as cheap, as last year's peaches, and Amy cannot help but think of her own family's meals and how everyone bolts down his food without a word, barely tasting it, as if eating were a chore rather than a pleasure. Still, Amy is amazed that such a banal topic proves inexhaustible and that even slim Cécile who looks as if she ate nothing but celery stalks, joins in the conversation with enthusiasm and eats twice as much as Amy ever does.

In her hiking boots, Cécile's slender legs look thinner, longer. Also, she is wearing short shorts.

Amy is wearing jeans.

"Where are we going?" she asks. Then, since Cécile does not answer, Amy says, "I love to walk."

Early afternoon in early July, the road that runs through the village of Rossinière is almost deserted—too soon in the season yet for tourists—only an occasional car passes them. Most of the cars in Switzerland, Amy has noticed, are red—perhaps to match the geraniums, she thinks. The window boxes of the chalets in Rossinière are filled with geraniums, the blossoms are full, large. Gladiola, peonies still, sweet peas, snapdragons, and weedless rows of vegetables fill the gardens that border the road. In the last garden, an old woman dressed entirely in black is hoeing. Slowly, she straightens herself up and, leaning against her hoe, she watches the two girls, Amy and Cécile, walk past. No one says a word.

"I like your hair. Really, I do," Amy says to Cécile.

Before Amy has a chance to say anything else, a car drives up—no exception, the car is red—slows down, stops, honks. The young woman sitting next to the driver rolls down her window and gestures with her hand. For a moment, Amy thinks she and the driver are friends of Cécile, but Amy can see out of the corner of her eye that Cécile has raised a strand of the barbed-wire fence that runs alongside the road and is crawling underneath it into the adjoining field.

"Ici, est-ce bien la route pour—" the young woman calls out to Amy in halting French.

"Excusez-moi, Mademoiselle, mais nous sommes bien sur la route de—" the young woman tries again a little louder while Amy continues to stare at her. No mistaking the young woman's accent.

"Cécile—" Amy starts to call out before she turns away. She can feel the eyes of the couple in the car on her as she crawls awkwardly under the fence. A barb snags the sweater she has tied over her shoulders, the wool tears as Amy pulls it free.

Cécile is halfway across the field.

"Who were those people?" Cécile asks Amy when Amy catches up to her. "Tourists," she says before Amy can reply.

The field has not yet been mowed and it is filled with tall grasses and Queen Anne's lace. The Queen Anne's lace reaches up nearly to Amy's knees, idly she reaches down and touches the tops of the flowers as she walks. Some of the flowers are pink. She is tempted to stop, to pick them. Ahead of her, Cécile has started to sing a song Amy recognizes immediately.

"Like no other lover—" Cécile's voice is loud, mock-impassioned, her accent even more pronounced.

"Something in the way he moves—" Amy starts to sing along with her.

"I love the Beatles," Cécile tells Amy when they are finished singing.

"It's a great song," Amy agrees. She has almost forgiven Cécile.

In front of them, at the far edge of the field filled with Queen Anne's lace, tall dark pines rise almost parallel to the side of the mountain.

Following the path up through the trees, Amy walks directly behind Cécile. The blue sky overhead is hidden from view by the tall dark pines and, except for the occasional snapping of a branch underfoot, it is quiet. Amy is amazed how quickly the countryside has changed—twenty minutes from the village of Rossinière with its red geraniums, and they are in no-man's-land, as remote, Amy thinks, as a jungle. Above them she can hear but not see a jet, no doubt a commercial airliner, and she imagines the passengers in their seats, perhaps sipping cocktails and admiring this view from above, feeling safe as they fly over Switzerland.

Looking ahead at Cécile, Amy worries about whether Cécile has ever gotten lost on a walk. The dark trees frighten Amy a bit and it might take hours, days even, Amy thinks, before someone would find them, especially if one of them were to fall and break her leg. Cécile's legs would snap in a trice they are so thin.

Amy also wishes that they would talk as they walk. So far, Amy knows very little about Cécile. Amy would like to know, for instance, if Cécile has ever been in love.

Amy has.

Farah was a fellow student, an artist. He painted large abstract canvases filled with yellow bubbles. "Yellow is a difficult color. After van Gogh—" Farah had shrugged his bony shoulders, given Amy a sad smile. Life, too, for Farah was difficult. In America on a grant, Farah was afraid he would be sent back to Libya, would have to stop painting. Amy sympathized—it would be unfair. But when her parents found out about Farah, to hear them talk about it, Farah and Qaddafi were one and the same. Nothing Amy said could placate them. The angrier they got, the more determined she was to defend Farah, like a cause. Eventually, Farah did have to go back to Libya and Amy went to Switzerland—a neutral country. But from Switzerland, Amy secretly fantasizes she can go to Libya—it is a lot closer. This is a notion Amy clings to for her self-esteem and is not anything she has the courage to do.

When finally Cécile and Amy emerge from the trees, it is colder, windier. The sky, too, is no longer blue, but gray, almost white. Ahead of them, Amy sees a moraine of stones. The stones are loose and slippery and are covered with patches of last winter's crusty and now dirty snow. Cécile holds out her hand to Amy and together they cross the moraine.

"We are nearly there," Cécile says.

Amy stops both to catch her breath and to put on her sweater. As it turns out, the hole made by the barb is right over one of her breasts. Amy sees Cécile look at it and look away.

Cécile is pointing toward the rocks on top of the mountain. At first, Amy is afraid that Cécile means that they must climb up there. The rocks are steep, sheer. Then, all of a sudden, Amy sees something move. Then something else moves. As her eyes grow accustomed to looking, Amy sees several more chamois. Five or six of them, at least.

The way the chamois stand, flat against the rocks, reminds Amy of those extinct villages she has seen pictures of in the *National Geographic* that are carved into and perched on the sides of mountains—long ladders are strategically placed in front of dark doorways, windows, yet the villages look totally inaccessible.

"I was hoping they would be here for you to see," says Cécile.

Standing quietly next to Cécile, Amy watches the group of chamois. They were absorbed in eating—tufts of dried grass, moss, lichen growing on the rocks—but now, as if sensing the two girls' presence, the leader raises his head, looks around. Then, leisurely, not in any kind of a rush caused by fear, all the chamois start to move on. They jump farther up the mountain, first one, then the next one—the chamois look as if they are jumping almost at random, with no specific purpose except to keep in motion—from one sheer rock face to another. Amy can see neither ledge nor foothold. They float gracefully in the air, feet tucked in, head and antlers contained, and land lightly and neatly, daintily. Occasionally, a chamois dislodges a stone and the stone rolls noisily down the rock face.

Cécile nudges Amy with an elbow.

The last chamois in the group lands on his knees. When he stands up, one of his front legs does not touch the ground. The leg dangles.

"Oh, my God," Amy says.

The chamois's broken leg crumbles underneath him as he lands on it again. Precariously perched on his knees, the chamois struggles to get back onto his three legs; when he does, without pausing or hesitating, he jumps to another rock. Amy watches the chamois do this several more times—jump, fall to his knees, get back to his feet, jump again—as he tries to keep up with the other chamois. The other chamois pay no attention to him. They neither modify their pace nor in any way acknowledge that there is something wrong. It is almost too painful for Amy to watch, while, for the chamois, there seems to be no connection between his broken leg and his falling. He just keeps jumping—jumping from rock to rock is what a chamois does, like breathing, Amy thinks. Even if something were to go wrong with one of her lungs she would still have to keep taking breaths.

"I've never seen a chamois with a broken leg before," Cécile confesses to Amy on their way back down the mountain.

"Terrible. He won't survive long," Amy agrees.

And, in a rush of words, Amy tells Cécile about Farah, about how she met Farah, about how immensely talented Farah is and how he must be allowed to continue painting, about how her parents are prejudiced and have forbidden her to see him, about how much she loves him—Amy has never loved anyone else the way she loves Farah—and how unhappy she is, although as she says all this to Cécile, Amy does not feel so unhappy. On the contrary, she feels happy to be confiding in Cécile.

"I wish you could meet him, I am sure you would like him," is what Amy is saying to Cécile as the two girls emerge from the trees and once again start to cross the field filled with Queen Anne's lace.

"Shall we stop here for a minute," is how Cécile answers Amy.

Obediently, Amy sits down next to Cécile in the grass while Cécile busies herself picking the flowers within her reach.

"Last year, at just about this time, in July, a man gave me a lift in his car. I was hitchhiking. I always did—it's so safe here," Cécile is saying. In her hand, she holds several long stalks of Queen Anne's lace and she waves the flowers at Amy. "He was French, I think. Or maybe, he was Belgian, I don't know. A tourist." Cécile shrugs her thin shoulders and gives a little laugh, at the same time that she starts to gently brush Amy's brow with the bunch of Queen Anne's lace. Cécile brushes Amy's nose with the flowers, Amy's mouth, Amy's chin. "He was the reason I cut off my hair, afterward. I did it myself. I did it with nail scissors. It took me all afternoon, my hair was so long. My parents didn't know. I never told them."

The flowers tickle, but Amy does not move. Amy does not speak. Amy, probably, does not breathe as Cécile brushes Amy's neck with the Queen Anne's lace, and, lower down, as she brushes the place where the hole in Amy's sweater is.

"We'd better get home," Cécile finally says, throwing away the bunch of Queen Anne's lace and standing up, "or we'll be late."

They are late.

Madame Cottier is both worried and upset that the dinner she has been preparing will be spoiled, overcooked. Monsieur Cottier is busy trying to choose the proper red wine to serve with the meal. When finally Monsieur Cottier has opened the wine, a Dôle, and they are seated at the table, Cécile tries to explain to Monsieur and Madame Cottier.

"You see," Cécile says as she cuts into the duck's pink breast, "it was my fault. I took Amy for a walk up the mountain and on the way home, we hitchhiked—I do it all the time—and this man gave us a ride in his BMW. He was a tourist, a Frenchman, I think, or, maybe, he was a Belgian."

Avoiding Cécile's gaze, Amy lowers her head. She, too, busies herself cutting the duck meat.

"He wouldn't stop the car when we asked him to," Cécile continues in an even voice. "He wouldn't let us off here at Rossinière. He just kept right on driving, isn't that right, Amy? Lucky for us, the barrier was down at the railroad crossing, and Amy and I opened the door—we were sitting in the backseat of the car—and we jumped out."

"Cécile," Madame Cottier says, "how many times do I have to tell you not to hitchhike. You never know what sort of person is going to give young girls a lift." Then Madame Cottier says, "It isn't overdone, is it? One must be so careful when one cooks a duck. One moment the duck is too rare, the next moment the duck is dried out."

"I told you didn't I how I am a twin?" Amy suddenly turns to and asks Monsieur Cottier. "You may not believe this, but you know how people are always saying that twins can feel each other's pain—well, it's true. One time when Peter, my twin, was away playing football at school, I got a pain right here," Amy touches her chest. She is warming up and beginning to enjoy her story. "I could hardly breathe it hurt so much and sure enough afterward I found out that Peter had broken two ribs and punctured his lung."

Without looking over at Amy, Monsieur Cottier takes a sip of his wine and says, "I should have opened this bottle earlier, I should have let the wine breathe."

That night, Amy does not sleep well. She does not sleep at all. Instead she tosses and turns in Josef and Marie-Thérèse Henchot's pretty painted bed. One time, when Amy opens her eyes she thinks she sees Josef Henchot standing next to the bed. With rough red hands that are more accustomed to milking cows, he is unbuttoning the row of small silver buttons on his short-sleeved black velvet peasant jacket that is exactly like the one Monsieur Cottier wears to dinner from time to time.

The next morning during breakfast, Monsieur and Madame Cottier talk about an old armoire which has come up for sale. Monsieur and Madame Cottier say that they have had their eye on this particular painted armoire for a long time—no one builds or paints armoires like this one anymore—but the old man who owned it refused to part with it.

"What made him change his mind?" Amy asks.

"He died," Madame Cottier answers, spreading more honey on her slice of bread.

The armoire, Madame Cottier is sure, comes from Fribourg; the armoire, Monsieur Cottier is certain, has never been restored, and never in all his years of dealing with Swiss antiques has he seen an old armoire in such good condition and the armoire, Monsieur Cottier also says, should bring him at least one hundred thousand francs.

When he finishes his breakfast and gets up from the table, Monsieur Cottier takes Madame Cottier by the hand and helps her to her feet. Monsieur Cottier puts his arm around Madame Cottier's waist, and, together, they do a little two-step dance. Cécile claps her hands. Then, standing up, she goes over to Amy and takes her hand.

"No, no," Amy shakes her head, "I can't dance."

Nonetheless, Amy lets Cécile pull her to her feet.

Second Wife

According to a statistic Helen reads in a magazine while she waits for Duane's plane to land, the second wife is usually two inches taller than the first wife. The article in the magazine makes no mention of the height of the second husband, and Helen wonders if this means that he is shorter than the first? And what about the third husband? Helen pictures a whole series of men becoming shorter and shorter crushed by the weight of yet another marriage, more children, more obligations and expenses. Meanwhile the women are getting taller and taller, because, no doubt, they are younger and stronger. They are blonds, too, Helen has decided by the time Duane's plane is parked at the gate.

Robert, Helen's ex-husband, had remarried a woman who was the same height as Helen, only she was younger, fitter. Helen would never forget how she and Robert had signed the divorce papers on a Tuesday, and Robert had married Margo the next day,

Wednesday. Since then, Margo has gained an enormous amount of weight—from her car window, Helen happened to see Margo crossing the street (Margo, thank God, did not see her). Margo, Helen guessed, has gained at least thirty pounds.

"You'll like her, I promise," Helen had been the one to say to Robert—ha! truer words were never spoken she was to keep reminding herself—on the occasion of a paddle-tennis game she had arranged between the two couples. Of the four of them, Margo had been by far the best player. She was quick and strong, while Jeffrey, her husband, was steady. Robert had played erratically—occasionally he hit a brilliant shot or he aced Margo and Jeffrey with a serve, but more often than not, his balls went out or went into the net, which, Helen could tell, made him angry. As for Helen, although she played a lot of tennis and was good at it, she had never played paddle-tennis before, and it took her a while to get used to the flat wooden racket, the underhand serve, the different ball that hardly bounced, the size of the court. The whole first game, Helen did nothing but say to Robert: "It's not like the tennis I am used to playing" or "It's not my fault if I haven't played this game before—"

Helen believes in the power of suggestion. How many times has she heard how a person, who, because she thought she could not have one of her own, adopts a child, only to find out soon afterward that she is pregnant? Likewise, months earlier and long before the paddle-tennis game, someone had told Helen that she happened to see Robert drive through downtown Charlottesville in his green Toyota pickup truck with a woman (clearly not Helen) sitting next to him. This woman, seen from the back had a lot of hair—a mass of frizzy hair. It took Helen a few moments to realize that the woman sitting next to Robert was not a woman at all, but their standard brown poodle, Oliver. Oliver loved nothing better than to go for a ride in the car and sit next to the driver, pressing up against him, so that from the back the two heads looked as if they were touching.

When, exactly, Robert and Margo had started their affair, Helen could not say—shortly after the paddle-tennis game (Helen and Robert had lost to Margo and Jeffrey) her mother broke her hip and Helen had to leave town for a week—but the day she found out about the affair was also the day she found the floor of Robert's green Toyota pickup truck littered with peanut shells. To this day, Helen is certain there must be a connection.

As for Duane's ex-wife, Helen has never met her. Nor does she expect to. Marie lives far away in another city, in another state, and Helen has only seen photographs of her. Photographs that Duane has told Helen he will get rid of, but has not. Photographs of their wedding when Duane was twenty years younger and his hair was darker, more abundant, and where Marie is standing in a long white dress holding a bouquet of lilies of the valley, and smiling. More photographs of Duane and Marie sitting in their bathing suits on the deck of a boat off the Turkish coast—Duane has described to Helen the cruise in the blue Aegean water, the archaeological sites, the inept crew—and photographs of the two of them skiing, again in a place that looks foreign (Helen can see chalets in the background). In all these photographs, Duane and Marie look young, happy, and Marie looks both blonder and several inches taller than Helen.

Marie has not remarried for good reason. Marie has discovered herself to be a lesbian, and although it embarrasses Duane to talk about this, Helen knows that Marie's companion, Teresa, is Hispanic—her family is from El Salvador—which might mean, Helen thinks, that Teresa is dark, short, perhaps even hefty.

Not as hefty as Margo, Helen is ready to bet. Helen could hardly believe her eyes at the amount of weight Margo had gained, and Helen has just to close them to recall, as if it were yesterday and not several years ago, how slim and trim Margo had looked on that paddle-tennis court—even though, because of the cold (February, the month Helen's mother had slipped on an icy sidewalk) she had on several layers of clothes—and to this day, Helen can describe exactly what Margo wore, how energetically Margo had run after the ball, how her serve had invariably gone in, all of which, no doubt, contributed to Robert's sudden infatuation. More than just an infatuation, Helen had to admit, since hadn't he gone ahead and married Margo?

Helen first met Margo at a luncheon. The luncheon had been given for the benefit of the Charlottesville Horticultural Society, an event Helen had felt obliged to attend. As it turned out, Margo had felt a similar obligation, and, leaning over in her chair she had whispered in Helen's ear during the first course—artichoke hearts vinaigrette—that, frankly, she could hardly tell one plant from the other. Neither could she, Helen had whispered back. The two women met once more, this time in a restaurant in downtown Charlottesville; they drank a bottle of California wine. From gardening, their talk quickly moved on to other topics, principally, their marriages. Margo confided to Helen that she found Jeffrey dull. Dull in bed, she said she meant. Oh? After a moment's hesitation, Helen had volunteered that she, too, was bored by sex—actually, Helen had never thought about whether sex was boring or not, to her sex was simply sex. Drinking more of the wine, Helen heard herself go on and describe to Margo how, in bed, she could predict all of Robert's moves: first he kissed her, then he squeezed her breasts, squeezed her buttocks, he put his hand in between her legs, et cetera, et cetera, and he never varied it. Helen had never said this sort of thing to anyone; in fact, she had never thought about it before, and even while she heard herself telling

Margo, she wondered whether she was telling her the truth. It sounded like the truth.

When Helen left for good, she again went to stay with her mother. By this time it was spring—the dogwood was out and the Virginia countryside had never looked lovelier. As the taxi drove Helen away from their—now Robert's—house, she noticed that the crab apple trees that lined the driveway were in full bloom and, all at once, she realized that she was seeing those crab apple trees for the last time. She would not be there in the fall to pick the crab apples the way she did each year, pulling a child's red wagon behind her up and down the driveway to put the crab apples in. And later, she would not boil the crab apples with sugar and pectin and make them into jelly. The basement of the house was filled with crab apple jelly jars which, in the heat of the arguments and accusations, she had forgotten about. If it had not been for the plane leaving so soon, Helen would have asked the taxi driver to turn around and she would have gone back and packed up all her crab apple jelly jars. Or she would have smashed them.

A few months after Robert and Margo were married, someone described to Helen—the same person probably who had told Helen about seeing Robert in his green Toyota pickup truck sitting next to a woman with a lot of hair—how, as soon as Helen had left, Margo had wanted to exorcise the house of Helen's presence, or was it Helen's karma? before she, Margo, moved in. Apparently, Margo had driven all the way to Richmond to fetch half a dozen Buddhist priests to come and chant and tie a red cotton string around the house—the string then had to be left to rot. Margo had lit candles and placed bunches of fresh rosemary, or was it bunches of fresh sage? in each room to purify it. And had it? Helen had wanted to ask. She was secretly flattered that Margo had gone to so much trouble to get rid of her.

As for the peanut shells littering the floor of Robert's green Toyota pickup truck, Helen has never made the connection. Instead, when she found them, she yelled at Robert: "Who the hell were you out driving with? A goddamn monkey?" Then, determined to show Robert, she got into the green Toyota pickup truck and turned on the ignition. She was either going to drive his truck into a ditch or drive his truck into a tree. Without looking behind her, Helen shifted into reverse and backed over Oliver, the brown standard poodle, who had been standing there waiting to go for a ride.

Oliver did not die right away. Instead, unable to move, he lay in the driveway with his stomach crushed. His eyes followed Helen as she took off her jacket to cover him, his brown tail wagged a bit, but that, according to what Helen was told later, was just a reflex action.

When, finally, Helen sees Duane walk through the gate, she waves to him. She stands up. She stands as tall and as straight as she can. When she kisses him, Duane's lips, Helen notices, are exactly level with hers.

Horses

The horses ran up and down the field as if they were chasing down a steer and no longer belonged to Michelle or to anyone. Her first night, they pushed open the gate and got into the garbage, into the garden, and trampled the flowers. In the next room, she heard Michelle get out of bed and yell at them.

"Git! Goddamn!"

The next morning, out the kitchen window, Carol can see them standing head to tail at the far corner of the field, and she feels as if someone had drawn in lines—the kind of lines in a textbook between, say, a tree and its shadow to show how perspective works—connecting her hands in the sink rinsing broken dahlias under the tap water to the two horses in the field.

Meanwhile, she hears Michelle explaining about her on the telephone.

"Was that him?" Carol says after Michelle has hung up.

Carol is visiting Michelle in California. She has known Michelle ever since they were roommates in college where they both majored in art. After graduation, Carol married John and Michelle went on to get her master's degree in psychology. At present, Michelle works counseling patients at a hospital in nearby Bakersfield—pronounced *Bikersfield,* she tells Carol.

"Bikersfield," Carol repeats.

And the job, Michelle also tells Carol, is not depressing, the way Carol or other people might think, on the contrary, Carol would be surprised at how optimistic some of the patients are and how strong their will to live is, and anyway, the hospital is where she met Kevin.

"Oh, Kevin was sick?" Carol asks.

Michelle shakes her head. "No, he drove someone in. A friend of his dropped a boat trailer on his finger. He chopped off his index finger. Kevin was there when it happened, he picked up the finger and put it in his pocket. The guy was in shock, Kevin said. When they got to the emergency room, Kevin gave the finger to the attending doctor. I guess that's what attracted me to Kevin—well, not attracted me exactly, but I admired him for doing something like that."

"Yuk, is that really true?" Carol says. "And did the doctor sew the finger back on?"

Michelle drives an orange pickup. Her dog sits on Carol's lap on the way to Sequoia National Park. His head hangs out the open truck window and his nails dig into Carol's bare legs. She can feel the dog's saliva on her face blown back by the wind. Instead of wiping it off, Carol lets the saliva dry on her cheek.

"Push him off," Michelle has told her, but Carol has not. She likes the weight of the small, warm, panting dog. The dog makes her feel less temporary, less like a visitor, as if she, too, might live here. Also, Carol feels well. She feels as if nothing bad can happen to her. She will not get cancer, she will not be in a car accident. She will not hear that harm has come to anyone she loves—not to her children, not to her mother, not to Michelle, not even to John, her husband.

"Huge. These redwoods are huge," Carol says to Michelle. "You know what else I am thinking about? I am thinking about John. Sometimes when I am away some place, some place different, I have this idea that if John were to see me, John would not recognize me. No one would. Not my mother, not my children. They would walk right past me like I was a stranger."

Michelle's arm on the wheel is muscular and brown. She drives one-handed, relaxed, and as if she likes to drive.

"I like the idea that no one can picture me here. It gives me freedom," Carol continues. "In Europe, I never feel this way, I feel the opposite. In Europe, everyone is always watching—I'm afraid to butter my baguette. But tell me more about Kevin."

Michelle says, "There's not much more to tell. He's like one of those leftover hippies from the sixties. He lives in a trailer, he chops his own wood, he smokes pot occasionally. He's okay."

Carol says, "You don't sound very enthusiastic."

"I like him," Michelle hesitates. "Maybe it's because you are here and I am seeing him differently. I am seeing him through your eyes. He's not your type, Carol. He's not anyone you would ever go out with. He's not like John."

"Oh, John," Carol says.

"You'll see, and his daughter—like you, she's from the East Coast—arrived last night. I've never met her."

"How old is she? The daughter," Carol says.

On the path through the woods, Michelle's dog trots ahead of them, and before Carol sees Kevin, before she reaches the waterfall and the pool, Carol can hear Kevin saying, "Hey, Max. Hey, big fellow."

Then she sees him. Kevin is bent over, patting Michelle's dog; Kevin is naked.

When Michelle says, "Kevin, Carol, my friend from New York. Carol, Kevin," Carol tries to look at Kevin only in the face, at his light brown beard flecked with gray.

"I've heard a lot about you. You're Michelle's best friend," Kevin tells her.

"Mine, too," Carol answers him lamely.

"Oh, and this is my daughter, Melanie—Carol, Michelle."

Lying on her stomach on a towel spread out on the rocks, Melanie is reading a book. Melanie, too, is naked. Melanie is eighteen or nineteen years old; Carol had thought Melanie would be younger, much younger—a little girl. Melanie barely glances up at the two women, but Carol can see that Melanie does not resemble her father—Melanie's nose, for instance, is more pointed, more aquiline—her skin, too, is smooth and tanned; Melanie, Carol thinks, is beautiful.

Max, Michelle's dog, is running excitedly back and forth on the rocks. His tail wagging, he sniffs into crevices, laps at the water inside them. At the pool's edge, he gives a few shrill pointless barks.

"Max! Quit that," Michelle says.

Michelle is already spreading down towels, opening up the

picnic basket. Next to her, nearly standing over her, his hands on his jutting-out hip bones, Kevin is watching Michelle. Unlike Melanie, Kevin is light-skinned. His tan is uneven—blotchy—his buttocks, his stomach, his chest, are much paler than the rest of him, except that Carol does not want to look too closely.

"Here," Michelle tells Kevin, "you can help me unpack this stuff."

"Does your dog like the water?" Melanie turns slightly to ask Michelle.

At the sound of her voice, Max trots over to Melanie. He begins to sniff her.

"What's his name? Max?" Melanie sits up. "What kind of a dog is he?" Melanie's breasts are wide and womanly and with one hand, she reaches out to pat the dog. The dog does not lift his head; he is intent on smelling her, as, full of purpose, he moves up along her legs.

Michelle says, "He's just a mutt. His mother was a Yorkshire; I have no idea what his dad was."

Max's head is level with Melanie's thigh, his tail is wagging harder as she strokes his back. Then, giving a little snort, Max shoves his small square muzzle right between Melanie's legs.

"Hey, no, that tickles." Melanie pushes away Max's brindle head and laughs.

"You want a beer, Carol?"

Carol, who has been watching Melanie, quickly looks away.

"Let me do that."

"All done. Sit down, Carol, relax. Enjoy."

Michelle has not taken off her bathing suit. She has pulled down the straps and she is lying on her back next to Kevin, her eyes are closed. Relieved, Carol has done the same thing.

"Bliss," Carol says.

Farther away and lying crosswise from them, Melanie has resumed reading her book.

"What are you reading?" Carol had asked her but she did not catch Melanie's answer.

"You guys are so lucky to live here," Carol continues. "I could lie in the sun all day. So peaceful. And I love the sound of running water. Some people don't. Some people say the sound of running water makes them anxious. The temperature too, is perfect, just perfect." As Carol says this, she wishes she could think of something else besides the weather to talk to Kevin about.

Less talkative than usual, Michelle does not even appear to be listening to Carol, so that staring up at the sky—a cloudless, stubborn blue—Carol wishes for she does not know what: John naked, Kevin dressed.

"Michelle tells me that you travel a lot," Kevin says to Carol after a while.

"My husband does a lot of business in Europe," Carol answers. "He goes over all the time. Sometimes I go with him."

"You're lucky," Kevin says. "I've never been to Europe. I'd love to see the museums over there, the architecture. And you know where else I'd like to go?" he asks.

"No, where?"

"I'd like to go to China. I'd like to travel all over China, go to Shanghai and Beijing, visit the Forbidden City, take a boat down the Yangtze River, but mainly I'd like to walk along the Great Wall. I read in a magazine somewhere that the Great Wall is the one manmade thing on earth that the astronauts could see clearly from the moon. Have you been, Carol?"

"China. No," Carol says.

No one speaks for a moment, then Michelle says, "Oh, I don't know what made me think of this but you know what *I* read in a magazine the other day? In one of those men's magazines—I read about a competition. A competition for the photograph of the smallest prick."

"Gee," Kevin sits up, "maybe I should have—"

"Wait, Kevin, let me finish. And you know what? They got hundreds of pictures of perfectly normal-size pricks."

"Is that true?" Melanie raises her head.

"Oops. Sorry. I forgot you were here, Melanie—but isn't that sad? Carol, isn't that one of the saddest things you've ever heard?"

Carol says, "That's pretty funny. I guess every man—"

Kevin says, "You girls want to go for a swim before we eat?"

As Kevin stands up, his foot knocks into Carol's leg. She opens her eyes just as Kevin steps over her.

The sun is shining directly on the pool but the water is so deep it is black, black except for where the waterfall falls into it, and there the water is lighter and a swirling green. At the opposite edge of the pool where the water runs down and disappears over the rocks, the black turns into a different color green.

"Cold?" Carol sits up to watch.

"Come on in, Carol," Kevin answers as Michelle, her face in the water, kicks vigorously and swims past him.

"No, it's not bad, I've been in already," Melanie says as she shuts her book and stands up. "You want to go in?" Melanie asks the dog, Max, who is lying on his side in the sun.

Poised on her tiptoes at the edge of the rocks, Melanie does a perfect little dive. Her legs tucked neatly together, her toes pointed, her brown buttocks clamped shut, in one swift motion all of her slides into the water with a single splashless ripple.

From the water, Melanie calls out to the dog, "Max, here boy! Come on!"

Max has stood up. Slowly, he stretches himself out on the rock, then, uncertain, he arches his back. In the air, his tail wags back and forth, rhythmically, like a metronome.

"Come on," Melanie calls out to him again. "I wish I had a stick."

"I'll get you one."

Carol walks a little way back up the path they came from through the woods. She got up too quickly, and because of the beer and the sun, she feels a little dizzy, a little unsteady on her feet. She also remembers how well she had felt earlier that morning in the pickup truck with Michelle. That feeling of well-being is gone.

For no reason she can think of, Carol is now reminded of spring vacation of her junior year when she and Michelle went to Italy to look at art. Carol remembers how excited she and Michelle were—neither one of them had ever been to Europe before. Carol also remembers how she had packed so carefully for the trip—all her best clothes—in a suitcase she had bought especially. An expensive suitcase. Nor will Carol ever forget how the moment they landed in Rome, their first stop, she realized, all of a sudden, that she had forgotten the key to her new suitcase. The key—she could see the little brass key in her head—was lying on top of her bureau in her room in the dorm. Carol and Michelle had then taken a taxi through a maze of narrow dark streets to a locksmith the concierge in the hotel had recommended to them, but the locksmith could not get Carol's suitcase open either. The locksmith said, or he said it in sign language since Carol could only speak a few words of Italian and he spoke no English, that he would have to break the lock, and Carol had told him: *No, mai, grazie.* Her expensive new suitcase would be ruined. So during the entire trip, the two weeks, through all of Italy—Rome, Florence, Venice, Verona, Milan—

everywhere she went, Carol had lugged her heavy suitcase which she never could open.

When Carol returns with a stick, Max is already in the water. Rigid, his head is pointing straight up, his legs splash water as he swims in an aimless ungainly wet circle.

"Atta boy, Max," Melanie says as she swims next to him. "Good boy."

"Come on in, Carol," Kevin says again, while next to him Michelle treads water and watches her dog, Max.

Carol takes a deep breath and dives into the pool. Her dive, she knows, is not as neat and perfect as Melanie's. At the last minute, her legs bend in an awkward split. Also, she does not know how deep, and the water, she feels in a rush that could stop her heart, is as cold as ice. For a panicky instant, her arms and legs feel useless; she is a stone and not buoyant.

When Carol breaks through, she tries not to gasp at the air. Her hair partly covers her face and the strap of her bathing suit has let go. Max is paddling next to her, and his soaked head looks shrunken. For all his thrashing, the dog is not making any headway. In the water, Carol turns away to adjust her bathing suit. To catch her breath.

Before she realizes that the water she is swimming in has changed color and before Carol hears Michelle call out a warning, "Carol, watch out! Don't get too close to the edge," Carol feels the pull of the current. She also hears Melanie say, "Maybe I should take him out. What do you think, Michelle? Max doesn't really like the water." Michelle's answer—"Poor Max is getting all tired out"—floats past Carol as she struggles to make her way toward the other side of the pool at the same time as she watches Melanie reach over and pick up the dog in her arms and swim easily with a one-arm stroke, the dog pressed against her bare breasts; even as Carol pushes as hard as she can against the water, she still watches Melanie hold the small dog and clamber out of the water. With the dog in her arms, Melanie has to balance herself with one hand to get her footing to climb on to the rocks, as she does this, she has to lean way over so her buttocks part, and Carol can see her pale anus and the wet pubic hair that hangs down in dark dripping strands between Melanie's legs.

Carol is all right again. Carol is free of the current. She can swim back toward the rocks and toward where Max is shaking the water from his coat and to where Melanie has picked up a towel and is getting ready to dry him. Next to her, in the pool, Kevin is holding Carol by the shoulders, he is saying something to her that she only half hears, only half understands, something that to her sounds like *whoathere, whoatheregirl* while, underwater, she feels parts of Kevin's soft flesh brush up against her, parts that she cannot identify but that she can imagine—the calf of his leg, his belly, his penis maybe—and that to Carol feel like useless appendages.

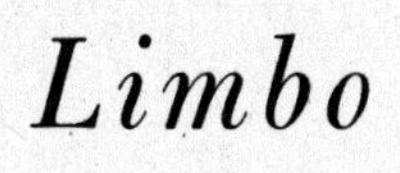

Limbo

What I remember about Peru is: flying in a plane over the Andes and fainting; stealing a statue of the baby Jesus; and threatening to eat a dog turd.

What everyone else remembers about Peru is why we went there in the first place.

My mother and I went to Lima, Peru, to wait until the end of the war. From Europe, it was a long way to go to just wait. A journey of several weeks—first by car, then by boat, then by plane. By the end of it, I was tired, I was sick, I pushed away my mother's hand and did not listen to her when, in between gasps into her oxygen mask, she said: "If you don't breathe into your mask, you'll faint." She held up mine to my mouth, but a few minutes earlier I had thrown up. I was afraid I would do it again. I held my breath for as long as I could and until I had to exhale. When I went to breathe again, nothing happened.

One of the stewards had to revive me. He gave me mouth-to-mouth on the aisle floor while the other passengers stared and my mother cried.

Afterward, when the plane was flying at a lower altitude, the pilot walked up to my mother.

"Is the little girl okay?"

"Yes, she's fine now. She frightened me," my mother answered him.

"Where are you folks from?"

My mother told him.

"You're getting off in Lima?"

My mother nodded. In her relief, she told him where.

"How long will you be staying?" Before my mother could answer, he must have remembered the war. "It'll be over soon," he said. "Is this your first trip to Peru?"

I was wondering who was flying the plane. The pilot belonged back in the cockpit. He had perched himself on my mother's armrest, he was talking to her as if he had all day. He took out a pad, he wrote addresses down. I squirmed in my seat. When at last he got up to leave, he patted my mother on the arm, he winked at me.

"I'll be seeing you," he told both of us, "and don't frighten your mother again."

"See," my mother said, her face was flushed, she looked pretty. "Next time we fly, you'll wear your oxygen mask."

The American pilot was wrong—the war was not over soon. In Lima, my mother rented a small house. The house was one story and shaped like the letter *U*. In the middle there was a courtyard with banana trees. I was very excited about the banana trees—I could pick and eat as many bananas as I liked. If she was in a good mood, I could convince the cook to fry them for me. I ate bananas until I got sick from them and left them to rot and attract flies.

Beyond the courtyard there was a garden of sorts, but the maid, Margarita, said the garden was full of snakes and my mother said that I should not believe everything Margarita said, but that we also could not afford both a cook and a gardener—to say nothing of Margarita. Instead, my mother planted red geraniums in pots, the rest she left wild. It was too hot, she said, and who knew how long we would stay. Any day now, we might leave, leave Lima and go back.

Back to where?

My father was from Berlin, and long before I learned that his house, the entire street on which he and my mother had lived, was rubble, I knew we would not go back there. Also, I knew we would not stay in Lima. Lima was temporary. Lima was in between two places, one I could not remember, the other I could not imagine. Lima was limbo.

The pilot's name was Jerry. When he was not flying his plane, he was flying through the air into the Lima Country Club pool. He did jackknives. The Peruvian waiters, trays in hand, would stop to watch him. He was not showing off. Once, I heard Jerry ask my mother if she wanted to fly with him. She could sit in the cockpit. After glancing over in my direction, my mother shook her head. Then, adjusting the straps to her two-piece bathing suit, she stood up and dove into the pool. Her bathing suit was red and white stripes. "Miss America!" Jerry called out after her. At the last minute, just before hitting the water, my mother's pointed feet crossed—like Jesus's on the cross.

I knew what they looked like.

Every day on my way home from school, I went to mass with the maid and I prayed to Him. I am not sure what I prayed for: maybe, that the war would end, that I could dive like Jerry, or own a bathing suit like my mother's. I remember that if I made a mistake in the wording or in the order of prayer, I started all over again. Also, I crossed myself all the time. It was more than a habit, it was a tic. I crossed myself when I crossed the street, when someone dropped a dish, when a dog barked, so much so that my mother asked me to stop. "It's meaningless," she told me. "You're not a Catholic." Since she did not say what I was, I continued to cross myself behind her back.

I wanted to outdo the maid.

Side by side, on our knees, it was like an endurance test: who could pray the longest, the hardest, without once looking up or at each other. Not much taller than I, Margarita had a flat Inca face and the heels of her feet were so dark and callused, I guessed she had more to pray for than I did. In church I copied her, at home I bullied her. Later, when she discovered the marble Jesus in my room, I bit her. My mother sided with Margarita. I had drawn blood and her hand became infected. "Why did you do it?" my mother asked me. I would not answer her. She asked me in Spanish: *"¿Porqué la mordio?"* I shook my head, I felt like crying. "You must apologize to Margarita." I refused. Margarita, red-eyed, and with an elaborate bandage on her hand, avoided me. I heard her tell the cook in the kitchen that I was just like a dog. The cook laughed.

We rarely mentioned my father. I waited for my mother to bring up his name. He was more hers than mine. Whenever she received a letter from him, she read the letter in her room, the door shut. I dreaded those letters. The letters were written in French (although German, my father had enlisted as a French soldier, a legionnaire, and under the circumstances, it would have been inadmissable for him to write my mother in his native tongue). My father's French was scanty, I pictured him with a dictionary in one hand, a pen in the other, and how did he sign the letters? *Je t'aime* or *Je t'embrasse*—endearments so unfamiliar as to be meaningless. Jerry must have been a relief. He talked to my mother about golf scores, canasta scores, not scores of dead.

My mother was twenty-eight, I was seven. At the time, I had no idea she was so young.

Jerry was older. Thirty-five, forty? His children, a boy and a girl, were teenagers, and at the pool, I watched them. Judy wore lipstick and painted her toe nails red. Both she and her brother, Jerry Junior, had adopted the arrogance and petulance of expatriate children. They read the local funny papers and ordered Cokes in a fluent colloquial Spanish that proclaimed their intimacy with the country, but not their attachment to it. A few feet away, their mother sat in the shade of an umbrella. She was either allergic to the sun or bored by it. When Jerry did his splendid jackknives not one of them looked up.

"Come on, Jerry, I'll race you," he called to his son from the water.

"Nah. Too hot. I'm tired."

I looked at my mother. She was reading a book, or pretending to read.

I will! I wished I could answer Jerry. I wanted to know what it was like to be with him.

When he sat drying himself in the sun, not looking at my mother or at anyone, I wanted to reach out and touch the blond hairs on his legs. My father always wore suits.

"I'm worried about her," I overheard my mother say. "She spends all her time indoors, in church, with the maid."

"Make her take swimming lessons."

It was a Saturday afternoon, my mother was playing canasta at the club with Jerry, his wife, and someone else.

"Can I shuffle the cards?" The hottest and stillest part of the day, I prowled aimlessly stirring up the warm air and American cigarette smoke.

"Can I cut the deck?" I liked to do that, which exasperated my mother.

"Okay. Just once." She frowned while the others fell silent.

My hands were sticky, I spilled some of the cards on the floor. Crossing myself, I bent down to pick them up.

Next to Margarita's and my church, there was a store that sold religious artifacts. Margarita was friendly with the salesgirl, and often after school, we went in there. While they were busy talking, I browsed in the store, I inspected the statues up close. I compared them. I chose which Virgin Mary was the prettiest, the kindest looking, had the nicest clothes. If I was careful, I could touch and no one said not to. I don't know when exactly I first noticed the baby Jesus. His flesh was Carrara-marble pink, His loincloth and eyes were painted the same aquamarine blue. He was beautiful. Precious too, He was lying inside a glass case on a piece of velvet. I wanted Him right away, but each time I approached the case with Him in it, the salesgirl broke off her conversation with Margarita. She told me not to touch the glass, my hands were dirty. Before I did, she must have known what I was going to do.

I could take the money from my mother's purse, but the salesgirl would ask where I got the money and tell Margarita who knew I had no money. I could save someone's life, another child's, at the risk of my own, and claim the statue as a reward. My prayers grew longer. I vowed never to ask for anything again. Obsessed, I readied my room for the baby Jesus. I concocted a shrine for him—a tiny bed of cotton wool. I festooned it with beads, I lopped off the heads of my mother's geraniums.

In a few months, I had learned how to swim well enough to start to dive. Jerry took an interest in me.

"Put your chin on your chest," he advised. "Don't look up or you'll do a belly flop." Sometimes, he would put his hand on my stomach to steady me at the pool's edge, then, gently, push me in. It was the only time Judy or Jerry Junior looked up.

Smack! I belly-flopped.

Jerry laughed, shook his crew-cut head. "Almost. Didn't I tell you to keep your chin down?"

I tried again. I was indefatigable. It did not matter that I was too little, skinny, and that I could not dive. Jerry's attention was like a blessing, his hand on my stomach bestowed more than equality. Over and over, I belly-flopped happily into the Lima pool.

One day, Jerry produced a dollar bill. I had never seen one before. "It's worth a lot of *soles,*" he told me. "See if you can keep it under your chin." The dollar bill floated up in the water, but it gave me an idea. I would ask Jerry to buy the baby Jesus. I would tell him that it was a present for my mother—she had admired Him in the store.

I waited for him outside the men's locker room while he changed into his golf clothes. The first time, Jerry came out with his foursome. The men were carrying heavy bags of clubs and laughing. Jerry did not see me. The second time, the men's locker room attendant came out before Jerry did and asked me in Spanish what I was doing there. When I shrugged my shoulders and did not answer, he said a bad word. I was tempted to wait for

Jerry in the middle of the fairway, but I did not dare. Children were forbidden there.

I was almost ready to give up when the cook rushed me through breakfast one morning.

"Your mother is giving a party," Margarita explained. "She has a lot of cooking to do."

I thought the party was for my father. The war was over and he was coming to Lima.

"If people ask you over to their houses, you have to pay them back," my mother explained. We were in the courtyard where the guests would sit before dinner, she was tidying up. "Wear your yellow dress tonight. What's happened to all the geraniums? There aren't any flowers."

My mother had lit candles in the courtyard and geraniums or no, it looked festive. She looked beautiful in a white dress that I had never seen before. Her long blond hair was swept up from her face and held up by a sparkling comb. To me, the stones in the comb looked like diamonds. From time to time, she touched them. Her arms were bare and brown.

"You know Ellie." My mother smiled and prodded the stiff yellow cotton on my back.

I was looking for Jerry. More familiar to me by the pool or playing cards, in our house, my mother's guests looked like strangers.

"How's the future champion diver?" Dressed in a dark suit, Jerry looked formal, forbidding. I almost did not recognize him.

The dining room was directly across from my bedroom and Margarita was serving. She was frightened of making a mistake and angering either my mother or the cook. The cook had taken a lot of trouble, for days she would complain about it. Kneeling in front of my shrine, I could hear the clinking of china and glasses, the voices and laughter of the guests. I prayed for Jerry to come out of the dining room by himself.

I must have shut my eyes, I must have fallen asleep where I was. When I opened my eyes again, I heard someone crying. My mother was standing alone in the courtyard, her back to me. Her shoulders were shaking, her hair had come undone. It was late. All the candles in the courtyard had burned out, the guests had gone home, the cook and Margarita were already in bed.

The next day, my mother searched for her diamond comb. I was determined to find it for her. On my hands and knees, I looked in the courtyard. Still on my hands and knees, I went to look for the comb in the wild part of the garden where the snakes were. This was where I found the dog turd. I picked it up to show Margarita. A sausage, I said. A neighbor's dog, a dirty dog! I was wicked to touch it! Margarita, beside herself, had screamed at me, and God would punish me.

The View from Madama Butterfly's House

Except for the nun, we are the only ones. The nun wears a retainer—the kind that is made of wire that comes out of the mouth and that goes from one side of the face to the other. Everyone else at the Nagasaki Museum is, of course, Japanese.

The nun is also wearing a short habit—well, if the a little below the knee length navy blue dress she is wearing with a white bib attached to the collar is still called a habit. A small gold crucifix dangles from the chain she wears around her neck and her head is half covered with a short matching blue wimple with white trim.

We can see that she has not cut off her hair—brown, light, curly hair.

A group of schoolchildren wearing dark blue uniforms is in the museum with us. A visit to the Nagasaki Museum, we have been told, is compulsory for them—the schoolchildren come from all over Kyushu island, from Fukuoka, from as far away as Miyazaki. Afterward, the children are allowed to play for half an hour in the neighboring Peace Park.

In addition to the schoolchildren, a young couple holding hands—perhaps they are here on their honeymoon—is visiting the Nagasaki Museum. The young man and young woman are brightly dressed in the latest fashion and each wears the same kind of expensive running shoe.

The Nagasaki Museum is not as big as the museum in Hiroshima, nor is it as modern. The Nagasaki Museum is four stories high. Each floor contains a different sort of exhibit. The exhibits are lined up in a row on the walls behind glass, the captions underneath them are written in Japanese and in English. The Nagasaki Museum is built on the exact epicenter. Before the museum, there was a prison.

There are two sets of stairs in the Nagasaki Museum—one to be used for going up, the other for going down. As we climb the stairs to go to the second floor, we pass three old people we have not seen before. The old people climb the stairs single file. They are holding on to the railing with both hands as if they were hauling themselves up out of a deep dark well with a rope.

The old people are no taller than the schoolchildren.

"How old would you say?" we whisper.

"Sixty-five. Seventy, at least."

"In 1945, they would have been young," we calculate.

A few of the schoolchildren are already on their way down. We guess from the way they push and rush each other that they are anxious to go out and play in the Peace Park. From across the other set of stairs, some of the children stare over at us.

Unlike the schoolchildren, the old people do not even look.

"Terrible," we say.

"Hard to believe," we say.

"Never in our whole life have we seen anything like this here," we say.

"To think, one minute they were on their way to work, on their way to school, about to catch the bus," we say.

"Children, too," we say.

"Madness," we say.

"And it could happen again."

The nun wearing the retainer is on the second floor looking at the same exhibit. Sometimes, she walks ahead of us and we can see her peer closely at an object, sometimes, the nun falls back behind us. Twice, we nearly bump into her.

"Excuse us."

We try hard not to stare at her—at her retainer.

The restrooms at the Nagasaki Museum are located on either side of the stairs on the second floor. The women's restroom of the Nagasaki Museum has two toilets—a Japanese-style toilet and a Western-style toilet.

While we are washing our hands, the nun wearing the retainer comes in. In her hurry, she uses the Japanese-style toilet.

"Ah, thank God," she says. On account of the retainer that she wears, the nun speaks with a slight lisp.

* * *

On the third floor of the Nagasaki Museum, the young couple who may be on their honeymoon steps quickly apart.

"They weren't even born then," we say.

The young couple is standing in front of a large wall clock that has stopped. The caption underneath it says how the clock face is miraculously undamaged, the glass did not break. The needles of the clock will always point to the same numbers, the second hand, too, has stopped forever between the seven and the eight.

The nun with the retainer says something to the young Japanese couple; the couple, in turn, smile and bow to her.

"Oh," we say afterward. "You speak Japanese."

The nun says, "I thaid how I was thorry. I apolozithed to them."

The nun tells us that it will be two years exactly next month that she has been in Japan, but that this is her first trip to Nagasaki, her first trip to Kyushu island.

"Our first trip, too," we say.

The nun says how, next, we must be sure to visit Madama Butterfly's house. The view from Madama Butterfly's house is of all Nagasaki and there is nothing quite like it, she says.

"We love it. The Japanese people. The food," we add.

The nun smiles and, for the first time, we get to see her teeth. To us, her teeth do not look so bad. Her teeth look like ordinary teeth, like normal teeth, like our teeth.

Now there is some kind of commotion on the third floor of the Nagasaki Museum.

The two old women are standing where we were standing a few moments ago and the old man who was with them is lying motionless on his back under the stopped clock.

"What is it? Where is the guard?" we ask.

Consternation lines the two old women's faces. We can see bits of broken glass on the floor of the Nagasaki Museum. First, we look up at the stopped clock, then we see that not far from the old man's outstretched arm is a pocket watch. A gold pocket watch.

Aii, Aii, Aii, the two old women start to wail. One of the old women leans down and starts to shake the old man by the arm, hard.

"Oh, my God!" says the nun.

The nun's lips are moving: *Hail Mary full of grace*—we cannot tell.

"A cardiac arrest," we say to her.

We look around for the young couple who is on their honeymoon but the young couple must have run down the stairs already.

Aii, Aii, Aii. The old women keep on wailing and shaking the old man by the arm.

Except for the nun with the retainer, we are all alone now on the fourth floor of the Nagasaki Museum.

The same man who collected our money and gave us the tickets downstairs on the first floor of the Nagasaki Museum had come running up the stairs with two men wearing white jackets and wearing plastic masks over their noses and mouths. The two men in the white jackets and the masks lifted the old man on to a canvas stretcher which they had brought up the stairs with them and which they had unfolded. Once the old man was lying on the stretcher, he began to moan.

"Oh, no, I thought he wath dead," the nun said. As she stepped back without looking, she put her heel through the gold pocket watch.

Aii, Aii, Aii. The old women had started up again.

"We had better go."

"We've seen enough."

"We are tired."

"We have never been so tired."

"Terrible."

"Nothing worse."

Anyway, we think, the fourth floor is not as interesting, the fourth floor is what happened much later.

Rue Guynemer

In Paris, she lived on rue Guynemer. Rue Guynemer is named after a very young and very handsome World War I pilot—she knew, she had seen his photograph in the war museum at the Invalides. In the photograph Georges Guynemer is leaning on the fuselage of his biplane; he is wearing a leather helmet with the goggles pushed up against his forehead, and he is looking resolutely away from the camera. According to the caption, the photograph was taken the day before Georges Guynemer was shot down; neither he nor his plane were ever found.

A little oasis, rue Guynemer is a quiet residential street located between Boulevard St. Michel and Boulevard Montparnasse in the heart of the Latin Quarter. The only store on the block is a bookstore, and the apartment buildings, like the one she lived in, are large and comfortable turn-of-the-century Baron Haussmann designs. The main attraction of rue

Guynemer lies directly across the street from it: the Luxembourg Gardens.

Every day on her way to classes at the Institut Catholique on Boulevard Raspail, she crossed the Luxembourg Gardens and walked by the tethered ponies and donkeys waiting to be hired out for rides, children sailing their boats in the boat basin, young men and women playing tennis, shooting baskets, jogging past her; and always she stopped a moment to watch the same old men playing a game of boules. The routine more than anything else made her feel as if she belonged in Paris and was not just passing through, a foreigner and a tourist. That and her dog—only dogs were forbidden inside the Luxembourg Gardens. The one time she tried, an irate policeman, his navy cape flapping, came rushing over and blew his whistle at her. Couldn't she read the sign? he shouted. The policeman bore an uncanny resemblance to her ex-husband. Or maybe it was his manner.

Her dog, a small, stubborn terrier, was also named George. Only she—the dog was female—was named after a writer, and the sound of the name when she had to make the dog obey: *George! Come here! George, I said, heel!* was harsher and less melodic than the French Georges, spelled with the additional silent and mysterious *s. Georges*—she liked to say it the French way, opening her mouth and squeezing the air between her tongue and palate then pursing her lips as if she was getting ready for a kiss.

In Paris, everywhere she went, people were kissing. They kissed early in the morning on their way to buy a baguette, then they kissed some more on their way to work in the Metro; at night it seemed to be worse. She saw people kissing—and not just kissing each other on the lips—in cars waiting for the light to turn green; a lot more people kissed underneath the bridges spanning the Seine, their embraces dramatically lit up by the *bateaux mouches;* they kissed in the movie theaters, blocking her view of the screen;

one night as she was walking George, she looked up at a lit window in a building on rue Guynemer and saw two women kissing.

Françoise Sagan, the French novelist—*très riche, très connue,* her concierge informed her—lived here on rue Guynemer.

Ah, oui. Bonjour Tristesse.

She had come to France for a change of scene and to learn the language. The fact that she did not know anyone in Paris, she told herself, did not matter. The beauty of the city would be enough, she would not be lonely. Strangely enough, there was no specific word for lonely in the French language: *seule, isolée, abandonnée,* she could even use the word *perdue.*

With George pulling at the leash, she took many long solitary walks in her *quartier,* going from rue Bonaparte to St. Sulpice, to Place de l'Odéon, exploring the little streets in between—a lot of the streets were named after French writers: Corneille, Racine, Crébillon, and Regnard—then returning home along rue Vaugirard where Scott and Zelda Fitzgerald had lived for a few months. Their building had large elegant French windows and wrought-iron balconies that opened onto the Luxembourg Gardens; also the setting for the Norths' apartment in *Tender Is the Night:* "high above the green mass of leaves." Each time she went by, it was not hard for her to imagine parties there, and Zelda, in particular, holding a glass of champagne and standing at the window on a warm summer night, looking out with her dark despairing eyes.

Georges Marie Ludovic Jules Guynemer was his full name. A slender young man with the same dark despairing eyes as Zelda Fitzgerald—and it was easy for her to imagine him as well. In fact, she soon had a clearer image of Georges Guynemer than she did of her ex-husband from whom she was separated less than a year. When she thought of her ex-husband—although she tried not to—she found it increasingly difficult to conjure up his face; she could no longer remember whether his eyes were blue or gray. The only feature she could still picture distinctly were his feet. Perfect feet. Jesus feet, she had called them. The kind of feet Michelangelo would have used as a model for his *Pietà.* One time when they were horsing around, her ex-husband, to show off how strong his toes were, pinched her so hard he left an ugly bruise on her arm.

At the Institut Catholique, where she went to learn French, the classrooms were airless and overheated and most of the students, girls working as au pairs, were a decade younger than she was. After class the girls stood in the street wearing their cheap new shoes with thick heels, smoking cigarettes and waiting for boyfriends. The second week, a Russian student whose long hair was tied back with a rubber band and who smelled of onions asked her out for a cup of coffee. They went to a café on Boulevard Montparnasse, and the Russian student—he spoke no English—told her in his halting French that he had left his family in Moscow to paint. He asked her to come to his studio which was on the opposite side of the city in the nineteenth arrondissement, and the next evening she took a taxi and did. Yuri's paintings were of ghostlike chairs suspended in brown air and she walked around his studio, which was also his bedroom, looking at the paintings and saying *magnifique* and *merveilleux*. Afterward, since they both could not and did not have anything else to say to each other, Yuri offered her a glass of red wine which she declined, then as if at a loss for what to do next Yuri pushed her down on his bed. For some reason she could not explain—except perhaps Yuri would say she had misled him—she did not resist him. She shut her eyes and let Yuri pull up her skirt and pull down her pants and fuck her. Later, the only thing she remembered clearly about the incident was how Yuri still smelled of onions and how he wore red bikini underpants—a *slip rouge.*

The two long blocks that make up rue Guynemer are intersected by rue de Fleurus and every day except Monday on her way to buy meat she passed number 27 where Gertrude Stein and Alice B. Toklas had lived. (On Monday, traditionally, the butcher shops are shut and only the *chevalines*, the shops that sell horse meat, are open, and when she first arrived in Paris, she had mistakenly gone to a *chevaline* and bought a pound of purple ground meat. At home, realizing what it was, she threw the horse meat directly into the garbage. The horse meat shocked her—she did not even consider feeding it to George.) Monsieur Lacombe, the butcher of the *Boucherie Fleurus*, gave George scraps and took the time to explain to her the different cuts of meat—he had learned a little English, he told her, when at the end of the war American soldiers were stationed in his village in Normandy. As a matter of fact, every year, he still received a Christmas card from one of the American soldiers, a soldier named Jack Patterson who lived in California. Did she know California? Did she know anyone there named Jack Patterson? Monsieur Lacombe asked as he chopped, cut, sliced the meat with efficient neat strokes. In the course of this, Monsieur Lacombe also told her how his family had been very poor when he was a child and how they only ate meat on special occasions, at Christmas and Easter. Now—and lucky for him—he told her, gesturing with a hand that was missing two fingers, people ate meat every day, people even ate meat twice a day. His wife, Madame Lacombe, sat near the entrance of the *Boucherie Fleurus*. She was the cashier. She frowned when her husband talked too long with the customers; she always referred to him as Monsieur and never by his Christian name, not even when he made a mistake and called out the wrong amount of meat for her to add up.

Monsieur Lacombe retired while she was living on rue Guynemer and his assistant, a young butcher named Jérôme, took over the store. Right away, with his pretty blond wife who wore jeans (Madame Lacombe always wore black) and high heels, he made improvements to the *Boucherie Fleurus*. He built shelves and stocked them with expensive canned pâtés, sauces, spices; he bought a rotisserie on which he grilled chickens, and right away, too, the quality of the meat fell. In addition, Jérôme, overzealous perhaps, cut off a finger on his left hand so that improvements had to come to a temporary halt.

Unfortunately her apartment on rue Guynemer did not look out onto the Luxembourg Gardens but onto a street in the back, rue Madame. *Madame qui?* she was tempted to ask. Rue Madame was so narrow she had the impression that she could reach out from her living room window and touch the apartment directly opposite hers. The windows of that apartment usually stayed curtained and shut, shuttered shut, and only occasionally, on a particularly warm and sunny day, were they opened. Then she was able to look into the interior of the apartment and into rooms that were heavily furnished and old-fashioned and were painted or wallpapered a dull green. She was also able to see the man who lived there. He was a small fat man and something was wrong with him. He would come and stand at the open window and idly wave his hands or else he would jump in place like a rubber ball—bounce, bounce, bounce—one time, she watched as he took down his pants and masturbated.

In addition to not being able to remember what her ex-husband looked like, she could not remember his lovemaking. Instead what stayed in her head was that she seldom came; most of the times with him she had faked it.

She was never quite sure how to pronounce Guynemer; she never knew for certain on which syllable to place the accent: *Guy*nemer or Guy*ne*mer or still yet Guyne*mer.* Whenever she told a French person where she lived or if she took a taxi home, she had to repeat the name at least twice and the driver or whoever she was talking to would invariably say: "Oh, you mean . . ." and repeat the name another way. Each time she thought she finally had it right, someone corrected her.

Georges Guynemer was from the town of Compiègne—at the American Library on Place de l'Odéon she found several accounts of World War I by American pilots who had joined forces with the elite French *Cigognes* squadron. As a youth, frail in health, Georges Guynemer haunted the airfields and studied the planes and their motors. He was refused by the army several times, eventually he was taken as a mechanic and he learned how to fly. It was not only his intense desire to fight but his coolness in danger that singled him out. It was not unusual for Georges Guynemer to fight six or eight or even ten combats in a single day and to return to his aerodrome with his plane so full of holes it looked like a sieve, his propeller mowed off by bullets. As the war progressed, he became still more unmindful of danger and took greater and greater risks.

For a few weeks after she had gone to bed with Yuri, when they ran in to each other at the Institut Catholique, they continued to smile and say hello but after a while they stopped smiling and after an even shorter while they stopped greeting each other all together. Soon, too, Yuri, she noticed, was arriving and leaving the French classes with his arm around the waist of one of the au pair girls, a tall Danish girl, and she could forget about having gone to bed with Yuri.

At the time when she discovered that her ex-husband was having an affair, an affair with one of her friends, she was both hurt and angry. Also, in a strange way that she did not even try to understand, she had felt relief—relief that she no longer need sleep with him. She and her ex-husband had stayed together another six months before they separated; during that time they continued to sleep in the same bed, and, at night, if accidentally she happened to touch him—her foot hit his calf, her hand brushed his arm—she immediately drew back from him. One time, she woke up to find him caressing her between her legs. Pretending to still be asleep, she let him.

By December the days had grown so short that when she woke up in her bedroom in the apartment on rue Guynemer it was still dark outside at eight o'clock in the morning. She no longer lingered when she crossed the now nearly deserted Luxembourg Gardens—it was always raining or drizzling. Instead, her head bent, she walked quickly looking neither right nor left, the brown leaves from the chestnut trees wet and slippery beneath her feet. *J'aime, tu aimes, il ou elle aime, nous aimons, vous aimez, ils ou elles aiment*—conscientiously, she conjugated verbs in her head—*Je n'aime pas, tu n'aimes pas, il ou elle n'aime*—were it not to signify defeat, she was ready to give up her apartment and return home.

Mid-January, a man named David called her. A mutual friend had given him her telephone number. A lawyer, he was in Paris on a business trip; he hoped she was free for dinner one night that week. "Which night?" she asked him, as if it made a difference. They settled on the next night, he would pick her up at eight. She gave him her address—she had to spell out Guynemer for him—and he joked about how, except for their unpronounceable names, he liked everything about the French, the food, the wine, the women. Especially the women, he repeated with a laugh, and since, she did not answer, he asked, "Are you there still?"

"Yes, I'm here," she answered stiffly.

When the doorbell rang the following evening, George ran to the door and barked. The dog's bark was high-pitched and loud. In the living room, she did not move. She was wearing a black silk dress with a low-cut back and she was sitting on the edge of the sofa in such a way as not to wrinkle her dress; also from where she was sitting she could see the front door and she could see George. In between barks, George was sniffing excitedly at the bottom of the door, her stubby little tail wagging back and forth. The doorbell rang again. Still she did not move. Someone called her name and knocked at the same time on the door. In a frenzy now, George barked louder. The bell rang a third time—a long protracted ring. It rang again and again. Then there was silence. After a while she heard footsteps leaving, going down the stairs. Very deliberately, she got up from the sofa and walked to the front hall. She turned off the lights and went back to her seat on the sofa in the living room. Curious, her tail still wagging, George came over; the dog sniffed her shoes and her legs, up and down.

Georges! she called.

She picked up the dog and the dog, at first, wriggled and squirmed in her lap, then settled down and began to lick her—her hands, her arms, her face.

Although highly decorated and a national hero, Georges Guynemer remained fiercely aloof and did not participate in the good-natured and slightly drunken revels of his squadron mates. About him one of them wrote: "the look on his face was appalling; the glances of his eyes were like blows." Solitary and obsessed with his planes—his last one was a Spad with a 200-horsepower Hispano-Suiza motor; his gun, the latest invention which fired straight ahead through a shaft in the propeller, thus eliminating the need to synchronize the shells between the blades; and, never content or satisfied with how many enemy planes he had shot down—his record was fifty-four, twice as many as Eddie Rickenbacker—Georges Guynemer, she realized, was a virgin.

Ouarzazate

At the start of World War II, my father because he was Jewish—partly Jewish, Jewish enough—left Germany. Most of his family went to South America, but my father joined the French Foreign Legion. He went to North Africa, to a town in Morocco called Ouarzazate. To me, Ouarzazate sounded like a joke. A bad knock-knock joke that I could never quite work out. *Knock knock. Who's there? Ouarza. Ourza who?* The answer did not fit.

After the war, my father settled in France but to hear him talk about it, Paris was nothing like Ouarzazate. The time he spent in the Foreign Legion was the high point of his life. Everything else was a disappointment. In Ouarzazate, my father had rented a house. I am not quite sure why—maybe the barracks were full. The house, he said, had no running water, but this was only an inconvenience. My father liked to talk about the real hardships: the forced marches, the rigorous discipline, the strict code of honor.

"We were like brothers—rich, poor, black, white—it did not matter. But at night, we had a good time," he added. "We drank a lot of Algerian wine." It was hard to imagine him. My father was not the dashing *Beau Geste* type. He was short and very nearsighted. As a child, I wished that he had looked different—taller, handsomer. Secretly, I hoped he was not my father. The hospital, in the prewar frenzy, had made a mistake or else my mother had had a lover. Whenever people pointed out that I looked exactly like my father, I refused to believe them. I thought they were blind.

In Paris, my father had to begin over again. He counted and recounted his losses. He schemed and struggled to recover the expensive Meissen china, the furniture, the Delacroix painting that had hung in the Berlin living room. His sentences began with: If it had not been for the war, or, Before the war, and the French tricolor that hung from the building opposite where we lived flapped in vain. His French passport was but a palliative. He would neither forgive nor forget. He refused to ride in a Mercedes or in any German-made car. It was not a laughing matter. "Don't tell me about turning the other cheek," he once told me. "If I had, you wouldn't be here." Not religious, he never said anything about being a Jew. I didn't either. I didn't know what to say about it.

"Being a legionnaire is like being a marine." When he spoke, my father's eyes gleamed behind his thick glasses—glasses as thick as a book. "There's nothing like it in the whole world." He barely looked at me, and I was relieved to be a girl. If I had been a boy or the son I imagined he would have preferred, I would have never heard the end of it. Or if the son I imagined was my brother—I pictured him a sailor—already I could hear my father saying to him: The navy is child's play compared to the Foreign Legion. And I, unable to resist trying to defend the imaginary sailor brother—he was blond and looked just like my mother—blurted out to my father, "But you never actually fought. You never had to kill anyone in the Foreign Legion." "No," my father answered me, "it was hard enough as it was. We marched all day long under the Sahara sun. The desert was hot as hell."

While my father was in Ouarzazate, my mother and I went to Peru; we stayed there for four years. During that time, my mother did not know whether my father was alive or dead. "Lima was hot, too," I wanted to tell him, "and there were earthquakes." I remember one earthquake in particular because it was on my birthday. I was seven and my mother, to celebrate it, had taken me to a movie, my first one. Halfway through, the theater started to shake. At first, I thought it was on account of the movie itself, the screen was jiggling with cartoons. Then everyone around me started to jiggle, to get up, push, shout, leave the theater. My mother was pulling at me to go but I had taken off my shoes. I was trying to find them in the dark, wriggling around barefoot on the dirty floor. "Leave your shoes," my mother had to shout. "There's an earthquake, we have to go!" Later, when the earthquake was over and we went back inside the theater to watch the rest of the movie, I still couldn't find my shoes. I looked around where we were sitting and under the seats but the shoes were gone. I couldn't concentrate on the movie after that. The cartoons no longer made me laugh. I worried about my shoes. I never told my father that story.

More than once, my father suggested that we leave France. "We should emigrate to the United States," he told my mother. "Opportunities there are better." My mother refused. "We've moved enough," she said firmly. "I never want to cross the Atlantic Ocean again." She was referring to our time in Peru. They didn't argue. I never heard my father raise his voice. I never saw him kiss my mother. He had left his passions behind in Ouarzazate. A bundle, they were fading and disintegrating in the hot Sahara sun—first red rose love turning a gummy pink, then fading to yellow, the color of old camel bones. Though older, I was still afraid of him. I clung to the made-up brother—I had named him Roland for reasons I have completely forgotten. No longer a lowly sailor, Roland was now a full-fledged captain in a spanking navy uniform with lots of gold braid. Even so, I saw his stiff shoulders flinch a little when he had to face my father, and my own heart sank. "I'm getting married," I had to tell him. "I'm going to live in America." "Is he Jewish?" my father asked.

"Tell me about Ouarzazate and what the house was like." I used to ask my father to change the subject. Already as a child I knew the question was like flirting. It was like asking him: Tell me about the women, the other women in your life, besides my mother, that you loved. "The house was an ordinary one-story Moroccan house," my father began. "Inside the rooms were large and cool—" He warmed slowly to the subject while I rushed ahead to picture a pastel house with plants and painted tiles—a Scheherazade house. "And what about the monkeys?" Unaccountably, my father shared the house with two pet monkeys. "Oh, I've told you about the monkeys a dozen times. The monkeys were dreadful. I hated the monkeys." I should have outgrown the monkey story but I clung to it—the same way I clung to handsome Roland. "To make matters worse, the monkeys crapped inside the house. One day I couldn't stand it any longer, I was fed up," my father said. "I decided to teach the monkeys a lesson once and for all." I had begun to laugh. "I waited until they were doing their business in the living room then I grabbed them. Both of them. I spanked them as hard as I could and I threw them out of the window." We were both laughing. I knew the joke by heart. "And from that day on, do you know what they did?" I nodded happily. "They continued to crap inside the house the way they always did but when they were through, they spanked their own bottoms hard, and jumped out of the window."

* * *

I jumped at the chance to go to America. My husband was a musician and we moved around a lot. We traveled light and fast. Then my mother died. The letters from my father were full of petty complaints, things he did not have. It was difficult to think of him and his long inventory of losses. I wanted none of it. I packed only essentials, like on a small boat. Like a sailor, too, I could hoist them on my back. I kept one picture of my father, a faded snapshot of him in the desert. In it, his hair is lighter—no doubt bleached by the sun. He is wearing his legionnaire's uniform and his puttees. He is holding a bayonet and he looks nearly handsome. "Why was your father a legionnaire?" my husband asked me once. The picture looked so outdated, my father could have been a gladiator. I shrugged my shoulders. "He wanted to, I guess," is all I answered.

It was early spring when, several years later, I returned to Paris. I was divorced. The first afternoon, my father and I went for a walk in the tepid sunshine. Still cold, he took my arm. He was crippled with arthritis and could barely walk. When we crossed the street, I had to hold up my hand against the traffic. As yet, he had not asked me a single question. Grown shorter, he looked wizened, a frail monkey himself. He must have read my mind. He told me the truth—the truth about the monkeys and why he tolerated them and their mess in the house in Ouarzazate. They were a gift from a woman. She was a dancer. "Was she Moroccan?" I wanted to know. "No, she was American," my father scoffed. "She was the loveliest woman in the world." He said it with such finality, the way old people make pronouncements, that there was little left for me to say. I invoked Roland one more time. Surely, in his peregrinations around the world, in all those ports, Hong Kong, Macao, Singapore, Gibraltar, he must have seen a lovelier woman. Roland did not bat a single seafaring lash. He, too, was getting old. All that wind and sun in his face had taken a toll, he was tired of confrontations. He didn't say a word about lovely women. "Was she on tour in Ouarzazate?" I pressed my father for more information. "Was she entertaining the troops?" But my father would say no more about the dancer.

My father died while he was making his slow, painful progress up the Avenue de la Grande Armée in the direction of the Arch of Triumph and the Tomb of the Unknown Soldier, poor old unknown soldier himself; his heart had stopped. About half a dozen people, mostly bent old men and expatriates like himself, came to my father's funeral in a nondenominational church. The service was brief. The organ stayed shut. I had planned it that way but the minister's well-intentioned phrases only made it worse. He had not known my father and the heaven he alluded to was featureless and for the homeless. I should have gone to a synagogue instead, a place more accustomed to wanderers. The only place my father had was a town with a ridiculous name in the middle of the Moroccan desert. Chances are the minister had never heard of Ouarzazate. I would go there myself, I decided in the dull church, and find my father's house. I would start immediately. Perhaps, I could persuade Roland to go with me: "You need a vacation, a change from the sea, like the desert," I would tell him, "and don't wear your uniform."

Next of Kin

When Karen and Richard got married—or right after as they were walking arm in arm down the aisle to the strains of Henry Purcell's "The Prince of Denmark's March" and out the door of the Greek revival church in a small town in upstate New York—eighty-nine-year-old Herbert Mirsky, who was on his way home from the hardware store where he had gone to buy fluorescent lightbulbs guaranteed to last a lifetime, suffered a stroke and lost control of his car, a light blue Honda Accord. The light blue Honda Accord jumped the curb in front of the church, and, because Herbert Mirsky's foot was pressed down on the accelerator, the Honda Accord gathered speed and sped across the church lawn—the car narrowly missed a hydrant, a hydrangea bush, and also, by inches, a maple tree whose leaves were turning orange and yellow—and nearly ran down Karen and Richard, who, oblivious, were just then making their joyful and triumphant exit from the church. The couple parted—Karen ran left, Richard right—behind them, the maid of honor missed a step and would have fallen if the best man had not grabbed her arm, as the Honda Accord came to a metal-crushing stop against the wall, at the entrance of Holy Trinity Episcopal Church.

Karen and Richard had felt obliged to wait along with the rest of the wedding party, the minister, the organist, the members of the choir, their relatives and guests, for help to arrive. Actually, two of the guests were doctors—an orthopedic surgeon, and an endocrinologist—and together, the two managed to get Herbert Mirsky, who was bleeding profusely from his nose and from his ears, out of the Honda Accord, and into the church vestry where they covered him with the minister's white cassock. Then, everyone, except for the doctors who busied themselves taking vital signs and trying to stem the flow of blood, stood around trying not to look but looking at dying Herbert Mirsky anyway.

In his short shirt sleeves with only his collar on, the minister looked undressed as he knelt next to Herbert Mirsky and prayed. The minister's arms were surprisingly tan and muscular; Karen noticed a tattoo on his forearm. The tattoo was in the shape of a heart, a bleeding heart, a name was inside it. The name was upside down, and Karen tried to read it: *Jesus? Janice?,* at the same time that a woman said something about administering the last sacrament.

"Poor soul. I've never seen him in this church before," another woman, the organist, who was standing next to Karen whispered back.

Richard, as if duty-bound by his role as principal player in the wedding, had gone over to try to help the two doctors. One of the doctors, the endocrinologist, handed Richard Herbert Mirsky's wallet, a cheap wallet made out of nylon and Velcro, and Karen watched Richard go through it. When Richard was finished, out of habit, he rubbed a finger along his upper lip where his mustache had been.

When Karen first started going out with Richard, Richard had a mustache. The mustache tickled when Richard kissed her and the mustache, Karen said, made Richard look like Dr. Zhivago in *Dr. Zhivago,* or more precisely, like Omar Sharif. But the truth was Karen preferred clean-shaven men; also she was afraid of offending Richard. When Richard threatened to grow a full beard, Karen suspected that he might be testing her.

"You don't look like Omar Sharif, you look like Groucho Marx!" Karen told Richard and Richard answered, "What's the matter with Groucho Marx!" But Richard had shaved off the mustache.

Now Karen was standing next to the crushed Honda Accord with her three bridesmaids—the maid of honor had sprained her ankle and was sitting down, her leg and ankle outstretched on the grass. The four of them were still holding their bouquets, pink and white roses and some kind of lilies, and Karen felt bereft and not married to Richard yet.

The ambulance finally arrived and Herbert Mirsky, with, Karen imagined, only the merest hint of a pulse left in his veins was placed inside it, and Karen and Richard and the others got into their respective cars—Karen and Richard into a limousine that had a sign with JUST MARRIED stuck on the back—and they drove on to the reception. It was only then that Karen noticed the stain on the antique lace train of her wedding dress—the lace train had belonged to Karen's mother, and before that to Karen's mother's mother. The antique lace train had a black tire track on it.

We could have been killed! Karen, each time she thought about the incident, said to herself. *We could have been killed!*

And the near-miss, she thought, was an omen. But an omen

for what? Richard, she knew, was not superstitious. If she voiced her fear to him, he would have shrugged his shoulders and answered: "An omen for Herbert Mirsky."

No surprise. Herbert Mirsky died in the ambulance on the way to the hospital. Perhaps, Karen imagined later, Herbert Mirsky stopped breathing while she and Richard were cutting the wedding cake with the raspberry cream filling; or perhaps Herbert Mirsky's heart stopped beating while she and Richard stepped on to the dance floor—in one hand Karen was holding up the lace train with the black tire track on it—to dance the first dance together: *"A trip to the Moon/ On gossamer wings—"*

Karen met Richard at a party eight months before, nearly to the day. They both, it turned out, worked at the same bank, only in different departments, in different branches. Richard was in corporate loans, Karen in asset management. When, after the party, Richard offered to take her home, Karen, it also turned out, lived only a block from Richard's apartment. The next evening too, on her way back from work, Karen ran into Richard in the grocery store where each was buying the same thing for dinner, a barbecued chicken—another and yet another coincidence—and coincidences, Karen had read somewhere, only she forgot where, were small miracles.

During the wedding reception, Karen tried not to think about Herbert Mirsky. She tried not to think about the blood coming out of his nose in brown clots and spilling out of his ears onto the priest's white cassock, soiling it.

The wedding day was a perfect autumn day: crisp, clear, sunny. The kind of day one feels one can see out forever—or, at least, see out for miles. A green-and-white striped tent had been set up on the lawn of Karen's parents' house. The tent overlooked a pond with fat geese swimming in it; in the garden, the orange, red, and purple zinnias, the tall yellow sunflowers, the more delicately hued cosmos were at the height of their bloom. Inside the tent, the tables were set, there were more tables with food and drinks and an oyster bar where two waiters were busy shucking plump gray oysters. A half a dozen smiling waitresses were going around with trays and plates filled with huge mounds of shrimp, a whole baked brie cheese, little sausages wrapped in dough, mushroom caps and endive leaves filled with dips.

Every few minutes more and more guests were arriving. The guests admired the view—the Berkshire Mountains, and rising behind, the Catskills—the guests drank champagne and ate the oysters, the shrimp, the brie cheese; the guests were smiling, laughing, having a good time.

We could have been killed!

Herbert Mirsky kept coming back to Karen's mind.

"What did you find in his wallet?" Karen asked, while she and Richard were dancing together.

"Whose wallet? Oh. Nothing much. His driver's license, a credit card, a couple of dollars. I was looking for the name of someone to call—a wife, a son, a next of kin."

A widower, probably. Since his wife had died, he lived alone in a small house on the edge of town. A shabby house, Karen imagined, with no garden, no flowers, an empty bird feeder hanging lopsided from the branch of a tree. The furniture, too, was old—the La-Z-Boy recliner in the living room no longer reclined, the brass double bed in the bedroom needed new springs, a new mattress, clean sheets. In the kitchen, the motor of the refrigerator could be heard laboring on and off, the faucet dripping into the old-fashioned porcelain sink; overhead, the neon light flickered giving Herbert Mirsky both a headache and a warning.

If I thought a bit/of the end of it/before I started painting the town—

"I found a picture—nothing important." Richard squeezed Karen to him, then twirled her around on the dance floor, in time to the music.

Instead of giving a speech, Richard's father, a handsome, large man who had been married twice and came from Italy originally—he spoke English with an accent and when he forgot he called Richard *Ricardo*—sang a song as a toast to Karen and Richard at the wedding reception. He sang without accompaniment and without using the microphone. His voice was deep and strong:

Some enchanted evening
You may see a stranger
You may see a stranger
Across a crowded room—

When he was finished—*"Once you have found her / Ne-v-er let he-r go—"* Richard's father wiped a tear from his eye for, Karen imagined, the wife *he* had let go.

Richard and Karen drove north for their honeymoon. On the way, the first day—more as a joke, a joke on themselves—they stopped at Niagara Falls. Several busloads of tourists were there. A lot of the tourists were Asian. Inside the Visitors' Center, Karen and Richard watched an informational film, then they walked hand-in-hand through the museum and looked at barrels. The barrels were stuffed with mattresses.

"You have to be certifiably crazy," Richard said.

"Listen to this." Karen had stopped in front of a barrel. "It says here that a schoolteacher went over the Falls in this one. The schoolteacher was holding a cat, a black cat. When they reached the bottom, the black cat had turned white. Snow white. Can you believe that!"

Wrapped in the plastic sheets that were handed to them, Karen and Richard took the elevator down and walked through a tunnel out to the Falls—part of the tunnel forked off and went behind the Falls, only Karen said she was claustrophobic. Instead, Karen and Richard went and stood on a concrete platform that overlooked the torrents of water that foamed and rushed and swirled down into a pale wet rising mist.

"Amazing, isn't it?" Richard yelled above the noise of the Falls. "The power of water!"

Karen shook her head. "Can't hear you."

Holding Richard's hand, Karen licked the spray off her lips liking the coolness of it. She thought about how easy it would be to climb over the railing and . . .

A niece who had never met Herbert Mirsky was the next of kin was how Karen pictured it. The niece lived in some place like Minneapolis and was not about to spend good money on a trip East. Anyway, for what? The niece's father, Herbert Mirsky's younger brother—younger by twelve years so that the two brothers barely knew each other growing up—had lost touch. Also, the niece thought she remembered that the two brothers had had a falling out—Karen tried to imagine over what? A bunch of worthless bonds? their mother's wedding silver? the family cat that had suddenly turned white?

Karen and Richard had hardly slept the night before—or Karen hardly slept—she had drunk too much champagne and the loud beat of her pulse inside her stomach kept her awake. That and the tap of the venetian blind against the window. Richard fell asleep instantly only to wake up around three o'clock in the morning, just as Karen was, at last, starting to fall asleep, wanting to make love to her.

"My Aunt Joan, you haven't met her, she lives in England and is married to a Brit," Richard was saying to Karen as they walked back to where their car was parked—they were both still wearing the plastic sheets—"tells the story of how Uncle Lucian—Uncle Lucian is her husband—went to Niagara Falls once, and a Japanese man asked Uncle Lucian if he would take a picture of him and his wife standing in front of the Falls, and Uncle Lucian, who had been a colonel or something during the war, said no."

"The poor Japanese," Karen started to say.

"Who knows, maybe the Japanese couple wasn't married." Richard made a grab for Karen, ripping the plastic sheet. "Maybe the Japanese couple were cross-dressers or transvestites."

Moving out of reach of Richard's hand, Karen said, "That's not funny and look what you've done now."

Maybe Herbert Mirsky and his wife had gone to Niagara Falls on *their* honeymoon. Maybe Herbert Mirsky and his wife had stood in the same spot and looked at the same falling water she and Richard had, Karen imagined. Herbert Mirsky was young and strong, his wife, too, was young, pretty; she was wearing a short-sleeved print dress. The print dress was soaking wet from the spray. With one hand, Herbert Mirsky was holding on to his hat, with the other hand, he was holding his wife's plump butt.

Her head on his shoulder, Karen fell asleep in the car while Richard was driving. When she woke up, they were entering the city of Toronto, and Richard, with his free hand, was stroking her breasts.

"You know the photograph I found in Herbert Mirsky's wallet?" After a while, Richard asked Karen.

"A photograph of what? A naked woman?"

"Two babies. Twins, I think."

The drive from Toronto to the lodge on the lake where they had a reservation took two hours. The land they drove through was farm country and the highway had narrowed into a two-lane road.

"It looks like Pennsylvania, doesn't it?" Karen said, at the same time as she wondered why she always had to make comparisons. On the radio, Carly Simon was singing a song about two lovers who had made the mistake of telling each other *everything*—the same mistake Carly might have made with James Taylor.

"So, how many women do you think you've slept with in your life?" Karen could not resist asking Richard.

"A million. A billion. I don't know. I'm still a virgin."

Karen had slept with about ten men. Twelve men to be exact—she kept track. Sometimes in bed if she could not sleep, Karen would count the men in her head—like counting sheep. She would begin by listing them in the order that she had made love to them—the first man, a French waiter named Jean-Pierre, she met in Grenoble the summer she turned eighteen and went abroad. Then she would list them alphabetically—starting with a Ben and ending with a Vint. Then, if she was still awake, she would do it by age—the oldest was her college roommate's father who arrived unexpectedly one morning while his daughter, Karen's roommate, was in class—she also made a list—that list was easy—according to nationality: there were only Jean-Pierre the Frenchman and Enrique from Honduras, all the others were Americans; the last way Karen listed the men was according to how good they were in bed. She did not like to do this. Partly because she thought it was crude, mostly because she was ashamed and did not like to think about the man whose name she did not catch exactly—the name sounded like Sandy—and who snapped gum in her ear during the two minutes it took him to—well—fuck her.

Richard was the thirteenth. For some people, thirteen was a lucky number. Richard was also the only man Karen had slept with who had a mustache.

"I don't know why this reminds me," Richard said to Karen then, "but my first date was with a girl whose brother had just died in a fire. A fire in a lodge, a fishing lodge. I was about sixteen and she was maybe fifteen. She was pretty, a blond, and her name was Lela—I'll never forget that. Lela."

"Did you sleep with her?'

"Wait," Richard said. "What I was going to tell you is that every time I opened my mouth to say something to Lela, I said something with the word *burn* or *flame* or *fire.* I just couldn't help it. Strange, isn't it?"

"Like Cyrano de Bergerac."

"Who?"

Lela. Or more likely Leah. Leah Mirsky, Karen imagined. Only Leah was not blond. Leah had thick dark hair. Hair all over the place—hair on her legs, on her arms, a large bunch under her arms, a darker thicker mass on her pubis. The hair did not bother Leah, even in the summers during the early years of her marriage when she and Herb went to the beach on Sundays, and the hair stuck out of her bathing suit. Leah did not swim but she liked to walk out and stand up to her waist in the surf, her sturdy legs spread wide for balance. She laughed out loud when the waves broke against her belly. The bigger the wave, the better.

Richard and Karen spent the rest of their honeymoon in a cabin overlooking a large blue lake. All the furniture in their cabin was made from logs—the head and footboard as well as the legs of their king-size bed, the bureau, the dressing table, the chairs, even the hangers in the closet were made in the shape of little logs. Over the fireplace, on the mantelpiece, there was a pair of moose antlers.

The first evening, Richard balled up and tossed Karen's underpants at the antlers and, all night, her underpants hung there.

Except for running into a few other couples along the paths in the woods when they went jogging in the morning and nodding hello, Karen and Richard did not talk to or meet any of the other guests staying at the lodge. In the dining room at mealtimes, Karen was satisfied just to observe them: most of the guests were vacationing couples; a few, like Richard and herself, Karen guessed, were on their honeymoon. The only exception was an older woman who was very thin and who wore a turban on her head; she sat with a younger man—her son? her companion? her lover?

Again Karen could not help making comparisons. "The couple over by the window," she whispered to Richard. "The woman looks like my high school science teacher, Miss Buttrick. We were all convinced that Miss Buttrick was having an affair with Mrs. Frazier, the principal." Or Karen said, "See the guy in the corner—no, don't look now, Richard—the one sitting with the older woman wearing a turban, he looks like Moira's brother. He's the one who made a lot of money designing a software program for pilots and stewardesses."

"I always fall for stewardesses. It's the uniform." Richard reached under the table and squeezed Karen's knee.

The woman in the turban reminded Karen of Isak Dinesen—except that, of course, she had never met her. "You know—*'I had a farm in Africa, at the foot of the Ngong Hills—'*"

"Yeah, Meryl Streep played her," Richard said. "Isn't she dead?"

"Everyone always mistakes Moira's brother for what's-his-name John Cusack," Karen also said.

"Oh, yeah? Well, someone stopped me in the street the other day and asked me for my autograph."

"You're lying, Richard—who did they think you were?"

"I don't know. Tom Cruise probably."

* * *

When Richard and Karen were getting ready to take a canoe out on the lake, they spoke to the boy in charge of putting the boats in the water. Standing on the dock, the boy gave them a lecture on boating safety.

"I've been canoeing all my life, since I could walk," Richard told him.

"Sure, man. I'm just doing my job," the boy answered. He was short and blond and he smiled at Karen.

Karen smiled back. "Canoes are awfully tippy, aren't they?"

"Come on," Richard said to her.

While Richard paddled, Karen trailed one hand in the lake. "The water is freezing. Too cold to swim," she said.

"You thought he was cute?"

"I thought he looked a little like—"

Richard splashed water at Karen with the canoe paddle.

"Hey!"

Karen ducked and the canoe rocked wildly to one side.

"Karen, keep still, will you!"

We could have been killed!

But the lake was flat calm. A gray-blue color. The shore was a solid mass of pines, evergreens. Karen imagined moose, deer, bear, hidden behind the trees. Richard paddled steadily, evenly, effortlessly; each time he brought the paddle out of the water, he flicked his wrist to feather it, before putting the paddle back in. Maybe Richard paddled an hour, maybe two, in the canoe, sitting up front, Karen lost track of time. She shut her eyes, she let herself go with the sliding motion of the boat in the water. For the first time since she was married, she felt protected, safe—even out in the middle of the lake.

"You know what I'm thinking?" she asked as Richard paddled the canoe back to shore.

"No, what?"

"I'm thinking this is the life."

"When I was growing up, that's what I wanted to be. I wanted to live outdoors close to nature and be a ranger or a forestry—"

"Live by yourself, you mean?" Karen interrupted.

"My father—you saw how he was—wanted me to grow up to be a typical American boy, not like him, I guess. I spent a couple summers at one of those Outward Bound camps," Richard went on, "you know where they drop you off in a boat by yourself on an island in Maine somewhere, and you have to survive for two or three days on just clams and berries. A lot of the kids hated that part. Not me, I loved it. Always, when it was time to leave and the boat came to pick me up, I wanted to hide in the woods, I wanted to stay on the island longer."

One afternoon while it was raining and Richard was asleep in the king-size bed made from logs, Karen went for a swim in the lodge's indoor heated pool. Every time she had gone by the pool, it was empty. This time the woman who wore a turban—except that now she was wearing a bathing cap—was swimming in the pool, she was swimming on her back. The woman's thin pale arms moved in and out slowly but rhythmically; a heavy gold bracelet sparkled when she raised one arm out of the water. Karen got into the water and began swimming the crawl, she swam much faster than the woman.

The young man—the son? companion? lover?—arrived carrying a robe and something else that Karen did not right away identify. From the other end of the pool, Karen watched as the woman in the bathing cap swam to the aluminum ladder and as the young man reached down and took the woman in the bathing cap under the arms and lifted her out of the pool. Only then, did Karen recognize what he was carrying. When the young man had strapped on the prosthesis and after he had helped the woman put on her robe, the woman raised her arm—again the gold bracelet on her arm sparkled in the light—and took off her bathing cap with a flourish. To Karen, the flourish looked like a kind of salute and she raised her own hand out of the water and waved back.

After the babies, the twins, died, again Karen imagined, Leah Mirsky became bitter and sad. She no longer went to the beach on Sundays in summer, she no longer stood with her legs spread wide apart in the surf, letting the waves break on her belly. It no longer gave her pleasure. Few things gave her pleasure—Herb didn't. Food did—a little. And she got fat. Truly fat. So fat she had to be helped into the car—not the light blue Honda Accord but Herbert Mirsky's previous car, a dark green Oldsmobile with a matching interior. Fat, then blind, then helpless. Every morning before he left for work, Herb had to help her dress, in the evening he had to help her undress; to save trouble, Leah stopped wearing stockings, underwear. Soon after, they had to amputate one toe, then two more. There was talk of amputating a leg.

"I wonder where they went," Karen said, looking around at dinner that night.

"Went where? Who?" Richard asked.

"The older woman who looked like Isak Dinesen."

Richard shrugged. "A rich lady on a little spree."

"No way. She had no hair, she had one leg."

"No hair? One leg?" Richard started to laugh. "Karen, what the hell are you talking about?"

"It's true. She must be very sick. I saw her in the pool. Everything's a joke to you, Richard." Karen was suddenly close to tears. "The Japanese couple at Niagara Falls. Leah, no Lela—"

"Lela, who?"

"The blond girl whose brother was killed in a fire. You think everything is funny."

"You, on the other hand, think everything is tragic." Richard put a forkful of poached salmon in his mouth.

"What about Herbert Mirsky? Have you forgotten about him already? I suppose you think his nearly running us down was hilarious—a barrel of laughs." Karen was crying. "Not to mention his dying afterward. Ha, ha, ha." Knocking over her chair, Karen got up and left the table.

"We have to make a plan," Karen told Richard on their last night in the king-size bed inside the log cabin overlooking the blue Canadian lake. "A serious plan."

"A serious plan about what?"

"About marriage."

"Right," Richard answered, sitting up.

Then he began to sing—*"Who can explain it? / Who can tell you why?"* Richard's voice was not as deep or as strong as his father's and at first Karen thought he was mocking her; *"Fools give you reasons— / Wise men never try"*—Richard was singing softly and off-key, and bending over to listen more closely, Karen realized he was serious.

Karen also thought about Herbert Mirsky. Chances were Herbert Mirsky was not a widower and he did not live alone in a shabby house; instead, at this very moment, a lot of people—his friends and family, all his kin, including the two babies, the twins, whose photograph he carried with him inside the cheap wallet made out of nylon and Velcro, and who now were a grown man and woman—were gathered together to pray and sing for him.

Hotter

Already it is ninety humid degrees in the shade of the mango trees that border each side of the road to Angkor Wat. Overhead, the sky is bleached white from the heat. I feel a drop of sweat slide down the inside of my arm, and my cotton skirt is stuck to the plastic seat of the pedicab. The pedicab driver, his narrow back hunched over the handlebars, is pedaling his bicycle rapidly down the dirt road; the muscles in his calves look like the banyan-tree roots that twine and twist in the jungle here. I turn my head slightly to look back at my husband, who is sitting in another pedicab, trailing three or four yards behind us. The drivers are racing each other.

In his high-school French, Peter, my husband, explained how he would pay the pedicab driver who won the race twice the fare. *Payer double.* He also gestured with his hands. Now, I can hear him yelling encouragement to his driver: *Allez-y,* man! Go *vite*!

I speak better French than Peter. I spent my junior year abroad in France, in Paris, and French literature was my major in college. I wrote my thesis on the poet Rimbaud. When I told Peter, he thought I said "Rambo."

Before we came here, I told Peter I was afraid that Angkor might be dangerous. I told him that I had read how tourists were robbed at gunpoint; that two tourists were shot. Peter answered that those tourists went to visit out-of-the-way sites, sites half-buried in the jungle. We, on the other hand, would visit only the larger sites, the restored sites.

Peter also said, Who knows what will happen next in Southeast Asia? We have to take advantage of this window of opportunity.

Besides our two pedicabs, there is no other traffic on the road to Angkor Wat. Only a woman dressed in a printed sarong is walking down the road; she is carrying two baskets on a long pole balanced across her shoulders. The baskets look heavy and bounce up and down as she walks. The woman stops and watches us go by.

Bonjour, Madame!

Without thinking about it, childishly, I cross my fingers. I hope that my pedicab driver wins. He is older and thinner and looks more deserving than my husband's pedicab driver. His shirt and shorts, although clean, are patched and worn. I imagine that he has a wife who squats all day fanning the coal flames, and too many children who have nothing to eat but rice.

My pedicab driver turns his head slightly and looks back. Despite his strenuous efforts, he is grinning. I sit very straight and very still. I also keep my legs that are damp with sweat tightly together. If I move them apart, my legs make an ugly smacking noise.

I think about what I might jettison out of the pedicab to lighten our load: *mes souliers?* But my sandals don't weigh much and my feet are not as tough as those of the Buddhist monks dressed in their saffron robes whom I see walking around barefoot all day. *Mes bijoux?* My wedding ring is just a thin band of gold and probably weighs less than an ounce. The only thing worth throwing out, I think, is the guidebook, which I hold tightly in my lap and must weigh nearly a pound.

The guidebook would land under the mango trees, in the bamboo thicket and among the lianas that border the dirt road. Pages fluttering, a few might tear off: *The palaces were built out of wood and have since disappeared; only the religious edifices built out of stone remain.*

Peter says that Angkor is made up from hard minerals in a paste of sand, and, since water dissolves this paste, Angkor will soon disintegrate. Peter should know; he is an engineer. He is building runways in a town in northeast Thailand on the border of Laos.

Louse.

Lay-oss, he corrects me.

Yesterday afternoon, during the flight from Bangkok to Siem Reap, the plane strained and bucked through thick gray clouds. Most of the passengers got sick; even the pretty Thai stewardess got sick. Moments before we landed the sky finally cleared, and from the plane window, spread out below us I saw Angkor for the first time. I had had no idea that it was so large, so vast.

Angkor has a system of canals and waterworks called "barays" that are as large as lakes, the guidebook says. *The area is over two hundred square miles and once included six hundred monuments.*

I turn my head again to have another look. Now it seems as if the pedicab with my husband in it is catching up. The distance between us is only a few feet. I am able to read the time, upside down—nine-twenty—on the watch around my husband's pedicab driver's wrist. My husband is laughing as he waves at me in a familiar and triumphant way.

Perspiring and stopping often to catch our breath, we climb the narrow steep crumbling steps that lead us up to the three terraces of Angkor Wat. *Each step marks a stage in the solar cycle, and the terrace represents the tiers of the world,* the guidebook says. I am in front of Peter, and, occasionally, to spur me on, he taps me on the behind.

Don't, I say. Stop.

Giddyup. Peter taps me on the behind again harder.

When we reach the top of the temple, we have a view of the countryside, which is made up mainly of stone ruins and jungle. The stone ruins look like large piles of bleached bones, and except for a broken tower here and there, the stone ruins form geometric patterns—squares within squares, within more squares. Rows of palm trees with their high arching leaves mark ancient overgrown paths while, all around, the water in the canals, the *barays,* lies stagnant and still. I see a man fishing from the bank of the farthermost canal like a distant mirage.

The Thais sacked Angkor in 1431, Peter has the guidebook now. *The Thais conquered the Khmers and took the women back as slaves.*

Slaves, I say. You'd have liked that.

Yeah, Peter agrees as he puts his arms around me and draws me to him. He holds me so tight that I have trouble breathing. Leaning down, he kisses me on the lips.

Peter, no, I say.

Why? There's no one around. Peter kisses me again. Hmm, good. Salty, he says as he kisses me on the neck.

Peter, don't, I say again. Later. Not here.

I can feel him start to lift up the back of my skirt. I try to move but Peter is holding me around the waist and one of his legs is wrapped around one of mine. I feel him fumble with the elastic of my underpants at the same time as I can feel him get an erection.

Quick, he says.

You must be crazy. I manage to pull away from him. You want me to get pregnant?

Even here at the top of Angkor Wat, there is not a breath of wind, not a hint of a breeze.

Hot. With one hand, I make a fanning motion.

Peter turns away and does not answer me right away. Damn right, he finally says.

When we were first married, my husband wanted to make love every day—sometimes we made love twice or even three times a day—no matter where we happened to be: in the backseat of a car, on a blanket in a horse field, and once inside a closet, knocking over shoes. Now that we have been married nearly a year and Peter goes to the town in northeast Thailand on the border of Laos for a couple of days every week, he comes back tired, he says, and he makes love less.

This last time when Peter came back from the town in northeast Thailand I went through all the clothes he had thrown into the laundry hamper. I took his khaki pants and turned the pockets inside out. A few coins slid out of one of the pockets; in the other pocket I found a matchbook—the matchbook cover advertised *Le Bambou Bar*—along with a few wooden toothpicks and a crumbled white napkin. Carefully, I unfolded the napkin—would I find a phone number? lipstick? dried semen? I found nothing. Next, I picked up my husband's shirt. The shirt smelled of gasoline and sweat and of Peter's deodorant. It was still faintly damp and there were yellowish-brown rings under the arms; Peter's underwear was quite clean.

Something shrieks as it flies high above our heads.

What was that? In spite of the heat I shiver.

Kingfisher, Peter answers.

Who knows, I say. Maybe, it's the reincarnation of King Jayavarnam.

According to my calculations—his attempt now and the one

last night don't count—Peter has not made love to me in eight days, in over a week.

On the way down the steep steps, I follow Peter. I also cling to what remains of the stone railing carved in the shape of a snake. My leather-soled sandals are slippery and, unaccountably, my legs are shaking.

Along with me and my husband, there are two or three other small groups of tourists. One group is French, and I can hear their shrill voices long before I see them standing in front of a bas-relief which depicts Vishnu churning the sea of milk. *La mer de lait,* their guide explains—the ambrosia that bestows immortality.

Im-mor-tel, a Frenchwoman in a red halter top repeats in a nasal voice and laughs.

The Frenchwoman and Peter exchange a look.

Last night when we checked into the hotel in Siem Reap we forgot and we left the window open and the light on in our bedroom, and when we returned from dinner our bedroom was filled with moths. Not just moths, I pointed out to my husband, but all kinds of flying insects I had never seen before. A lot of the insects were caught in the folds of the mosquito net that hung over our bed, and even after Peter shook the net out and turned off the light, they remained clinging to it.

Don't worry, the bugs are harmless, he said in bed, pushing up my nightgown.

No, I said, pushing away his hand. My stomach.

Your stomach? What's wrong with your stomach?

I don't know, I answered, turning away from him. The noodles at dinner, maybe.

* * *

As we reach the bottom steps of Angkor Wat, we meet a Japanese couple who are on their way up. The Japanese couple smile and move aside to let us pass.

Near the entrance gate of the temple, a vendor is selling soft drinks. Half a dozen bottles of Coca-Cola and the orange drink Fanta are lying in a bucket of water. When I pick up a bottle out of the water, the water is warm. Hot, nearly. When the vendor offers me a straw, I shake my head. A bunch of flies are swarming on the rim of the glass that holds the straws.

Sipping the Fanta straight out of the bottle, I walk beside my husband to the next site.

Tonight, Peter, I tell him. We can make love in the hotel, tonight.

Peter does not answer me.

Two little boys are following us: *Hello! Hello!*

Amelican!

One little boy makes the sound of a gun going off—*bang bang*—the same sound in every language. The other little boy has something wrong with one eye; only the white part shows.

In 802, King Jayavarnam II founded Angkor as the seat of his kingdom. Angkor comes from the Sanskrit word "nagara" which means "city"—I am reading aloud from the guidebook. Are you listening, Peter? In a singsong voice and mimicking an Asian accent, I begin again: *Ankle koms flom se Sansclit wold*—

Yeah, sure. Bang, bang.

By the side of the road, slim columns of red earth rise several feet high. They look like sculptures and are the homes of termite ants.

Two rows of stone giants guard Angkor Thom, the capital of Angkor; the giants wrestle stone serpents in their arms.

I'll take a picture of you, Peter offers.

I straddle a stone serpent and put my arms around a stone giant's neck. I kiss the stone giant on the lips.

Great! Peter shouts. Again! This time a French kiss!

Your turn, I say.

Wait till I find another one of those dancing nymphs—what are they called?—the ones with the long skirts and naked tits.

Apsaras.

One day when I was not wearing a bra and, according to Peter, anyone who wanted to could look down my dress at my breasts, an insect of some kind—a bumblebee maybe or a big horsefly, I never found out which—flew inside my dress and, in my frenzy, I forgot that the zipper on that particular dress was located on the right instead of the left side, and I ripped the dress the whole length from the sleeve to the hem trying to get it off quickly. Peter, who was watching, said, it served me right for wearing a low-cut dress like that. Also, he said, it reminded him of a story he had heard once about a World War II pilot who had to parachute out of his plane, but it turned out that he was left-handed, so that by the time he reached the ground he had nearly eviscerated himself trying in vain to find the rip cord.

Each of the fifty towers of the Bayon is topped with four huge smiling heads. The heads have big lips and their smiles are full of mystery. The heads are supposed to represent King Jayavarnam, but they are too beautiful, I think. King Jayavarnam, I read in the guidebook, was a leper and became king only in his late sixties.

All of a sudden, as I am looking up at the huge heads, I feel dizzy. Nauseated, too. Except for the bottle of Fanta, I have not drunk or eaten anything since the noodles at dinner yesterday—not even the glass of weak tea that was left in our hotel bedroom which I used instead to brush my teeth. I sit down. I put my head between my knees the way I know people who feel faint are supposed to.

I have been careful—the one time, on a trip to Chieng Mai, I forgot to bring along my diaphragm and we had sex, Peter came in my mouth instead—and I always use some form of protection, but should I get pregnant here Peter has promised me that I can go home. I can stay with my parents, he has said, and wait there for the baby. Sometimes at night, after we have finished making love and Peter has already turned over and I can hear him snoring lightly and I am too hot still and cannot sleep, I try to imagine that the geckos I hear crawling on the window screens are crickets. I try to imagine that the frangipani tree outside the bedroom window with its cloying, too-sweet blossoms is the sturdy maple tree in my parents' garden. I try to imagine what it would be like to sleep under a warm goose-down quilt in a single bed again, what it would be like to feel cool, cold even. But trying to imagine this always defeats me.

What are you doing anyway, Anne? Peter asks. He is frowning. He is sitting on top of a fallen pillar, and has taken off one of his sneakers.

Nothing, I answer.

I got bitten by something, he says. He holds up his foot to me. See. It hurts like hell, he says. A red ant.

Maybe the ant is the reincarnation of King Jayavarnam—I start again.

Anne! Do you mind shutting up about King Jaya-what-his-face? It takes only a dozen or so of these ant bites to kill an average-size man.

Hotter.

A blue butterfly hovers and alights for a moment on one of the stone head's big smiling lips.

Him! I think.

* * *

As we are leaving Angkor Thom, I look over my shoulder.

Can you quit that? Peter says. You're giving me the creeps. The next temple isn't far. Just over there.

The path has turned into an overgrown track full of ruts; in some places we have to walk single file. I try to stay within Peter's diminishing shadow; I try to step on his back, on his head.

I don't know. It looks kind of deserted here. What's it called? I ask as I look up the site in the guidebook.

Preah Khan.

Preah Khan? The guidebook says that Preah Khan is not one of the restored sites, I tell my husband. Preah Khan is an unrestored site. I don't see anyone else going there, I also tell him. I'm worried—

Anne, that's your trouble. Peter stops for a moment and puts his arm around me. Relax, will you.

I shrug his arm off.

During my junior year abroad, I went to Normandy with a boy named Jean-Claude. Jean-Claude and I took the train from Paris to Cherbourg, and there we rented bicycles. We planned to cycle along the coast, camp out in farmers' fields, and look at the beaches. The first day, on Omaha Beach, we clambered on top of an abandoned rusty tank, then Jean-Claude climbed down inside one of the bunkers. I remember how I would not go with him, I said I was afraid of a live grenade still. Jean-Claude stayed in the bunker for such a long time that I began to worry about him. When, finally, he emerged, we walked back up the beach to where there was a monument. The monument was in the shape of an obelisk and was set on top of some granite steps; the granite was warm from the sun and we sat down. Also, by then we were hungry. Jean-Claude and I opened our backpacks and spread out the salami, bread, cheese, and wine we had bought for lunch. After we had eaten the bread, salami, and cheese and drunk the wine, we lay down on the steps and Jean-Claude began to kiss me. I closed my eyes and I still remember how Jean-Claude's kisses tasted of warm red wine, rust, and the sea. Then, just as Jean-Claude was starting to unbutton my blouse, I heard someone run up the granite steps and yell at us: *Mais, alors! N'avez vous aucun respect pour les morts!*

The Gate of Victory, the name of the gate through which we enter, is surmounted by a tower with four more smiling heads of King Jayavarnam. A banyan tree has grown over the tower and a tangled network of roots and branches have completely encircled the huge stone heads—breaking off a nose, mashing an ear, blinding an eye, turning the smile of the old leper king into a sneer.

Look, Peter points. You can see the brick underneath the sandstone. You can see the original corbeling.

Inside the unrestored temple, we have to step over fallen lintels, stones, pillars. Another banyan tree has spread its roots, cracking the floor, toppling the roof.

See the original what? I ask, as a troupe of gibbons leaps into the branches directly over our heads; the gibbons shake the foliage and chatter down at us: *Whoop, whoop, whoop.*

Something small and hard hits me on the cheek.

Hey!

Then more nuts start to rain down, hitting me and my husband. Peter leans down on the ground and picks up a handful of nuts; he starts throwing the nuts back at the gibbons.

Goddamn monkeys! he yells.

On the way back to Siem Reap in the pedicabs—this time the drivers are pedaling slowly and not racing each other—we suddenly hear yelping. The yelping comes from the bamboo thickets and lianas that border the side of the road and to me it sounds pitiful and like a baby crying almost.

Stop! I lean forward and tell the pedicab driver. *Arrêtez!* We have to stop!

Likewise, my husband motions to his pedicab driver and we both get out of the pedicabs.

Be careful, I say.

Our drivers do not appear concerned; my pedicab driver is cleaning his ear with his fingernail—the pinkie fingernail grown long expressly for that purpose.

Oh, God! As if to stop me, my husband holds out his hand.

What is it? I ask.

It takes me several seconds to understand what I am looking at: two mongrel dogs are stuck together. The male dog is making awkward plunging motions while the female dog has gotten herself grotesquely twisted around and is being dragged along on her bony back; between her legs, what is visible of the male dog's penis is a glistening bright red.

Once again, I feel dizzy. I can taste the Fanta rising up in my throat.

In their frenzy, both dogs are also biting at each other. The female dog, the dog that is being dragged on her back, I notice, has bitten herself. Her tongue is full of little marks, little bloody tooth marks. The yelping, we heard, however, has stopped.

Dream House

Sometimes Isabel dreams she goes back to a house she has never lived in or set foot in. Yet the moment she opens the front door, the moment she enters the front hall, everything seems familiar and, in the dream, she feels enormous relief. They are back together again. For a trial period. Her former husband is very subdued, he does not shout or tell stories in his booming loud voice; when he kisses her he kisses her on the cheek, not on the mouth. Also, he does not make any sexual advances. It is she now in the dream who flirts with him. When she speaks to him she puts her hand on his arm for an unnecessarily long time, she bumps into him accidentally-on-purpose with her hip; she sighs a lot, she leaves the top buttons of her blouse unbuttoned. In bed, she turns from side to side dissatisfied and unable to go to sleep while, next to her, her former husband lies flat on his back and snores evenly, peacefully.

The first house Sam and Isabel lived in together was not a house but a boat. A thirty-four-foot ketch named *Eudora*. They had planned to sail around the world or cross the Atlantic Ocean but they only got as far as the Caribbean where they stayed a year, island hopping and living the ideal, dreamed-of, carefree life: cooking fresh-caught fish, eating fresh-picked fruit, every day wearing the same clothes—Isabel wore a bikini bathing suit, if the wind picked up, she put on a T-shirt. Every day, too, they dove off the deck of the boat and swam for hours in the warm aquamarine water. At night, they made love rocking to the motion of the boat at anchor and listening to the slap-slap sound of the waves against the boat's hull; if it got too hot down below, they slept on deck under the stars whose names and positions in the sky Isabel got to know by heart.

They were fortunate too, they never got into really bad weather—a few sudden tropical squalls that made the boat heel way over and the keel shudder and groan and that caused all the gear that was not tied down or not put away to roll noisily to the floor. One time when they were sailing around the island of Puerto Rico, they got becalmed—the sea was full of floating bunches of seaweed, the reason perhaps the motor did not start—and for a while they drifted so close to the coast that Isabel claimed she could identify, with her naked eye, the laundry hanging out to dry in someone's yard: *"Mira, mira,"* she sang out, "two pairs of jeans, four white shirts, two bras, one red blouse."

"Come on, baby!" Sam was not listening to Isabel. He seesawed the tiller back and forth trying to create some momentum so they could come about.

Sam loved the *Eudora*—"honey," "sweetheart," was how he talked to the boat. He scrubbed *Eudora*'s teak deck with a holystone, he polished her brass until it sparkled. He liked keeping everything on board shipshape, the sheets coiled, the winch handles stowed, he liked for nothing—Isabel could not leave even a sweater lying on deck—to be out of place.

"I learned my lesson the hard way," Sam told her. "One summer when I was a kid and I was cruising up in Nova Scotia with my uncle, I left my brand-new Top-Siders lying on the deck and my uncle found them and he held up the Top-Siders and asked: 'Whose shoes?' When I answered, 'Gee, thanks, they're mine,' my uncle tossed my Top-Siders overboard. But he got his comeuppance," Sam continued. "A few days later I found his Rolex watch inside the head. He had forgotten it there. I held up the Rolex watch and said: 'Whose watch?' and my uncle went: 'Gee, thanks, that's my watch,' and, guess what, I dropped the Rolex watch in the ocean."

"I can't believe you did that," Isabel said.

And "Captain's word is law," Sam also liked to tell her especially when they were lying in their double bunk in the bow of the boat and he was putting Isabel on top of him.

The first time Isabel saw Sam, he was standing in the middle of a group of people and he was telling them a story. A story Isabel could hear clear across the room about how one of his relatives—Sam came from a large family of sailors—had sailed alone across the Atlantic Ocean and every evening at six o'clock sharp no matter what the weather was like, even if the wind was gusting at thirty knots and the waves were ten feet high, he went down below and put on a coat and tie and made himself a martini. Everyone, including Sam, laughed, but Isabel stepped in. "I don't believe you," she said.

"It's true, I promise you." Still laughing, Sam looked Isabel over. "A gimlet martini."

Usually they stayed only a couple of days on each island: Eleuthera, Nassau, a few of the Virgin Islands, Antigua, Barbuda, St. Kitts; but they stayed nearly a month in Jamaica. They anchored out in Montego Bay and every day they hitchhiked to Negril, a two-mile-long sandy beach filled with kids. Sam and Isabel didn't do anything special: they smoked a little pot, they drank rum, they lay in the sun and got free massages on the beach; also they met Neil.

Like Sam and Isabel, Neil was in his early twenties and bumming around the Caribbean. He had worked on a couple of charters and had stories about the goings-on on board. Stories of how the couples drank too much and switched partners and how one time when they were anchored off Barbados, one couple went skinny-dipping in the middle of the night only the couple forgot to put down the ladder so when they tried to get out of the water and back on board they couldn't. Apparently, the couple shouted and yelled and splashed water against the portholes before finally Neil woke up—everyone else he claimed was too drunk—and he helped them climb back in the boat.

"I should have just let them drown or get eaten by sharks," Neil said. "You should have seen them—the man's dick had withered to nothing, the woman's breasts came down to here." Neil pointed to his knees.

Isabel said, "They could have swum to shore."

"Yeah, and then what? How would you like to be wandering around the island of Barbados in the middle of the night stark naked?"

The three laughed at the idea of it. But, like a bad dream, the image stayed in Isabel's head. She could see the middle-aged couple stumbling around on the dark beach, shivering and trying to hide their nakedness with their hands, then walking to a house where there still was a light and knocking on the door and a dog barking. The man would be murdered, the woman raped and then murdered.

Isabel does not remember who asked him—or, more likely, Neil asked them—but Neil went with Sam and Isabel from Jamaica to St. Thomas, where the charter company he worked for sailed from. Once on board the *Eudora*, Neil's stories no longer seemed funny and, worse, Neil's presence seemed in some way to pollute the atmosphere. Neither Sam nor Isabel spoke of this but while Neil was talking, Sam and Isabel avoided each other's eyes and looked out at some distant point on the horizon. Often too, when Neil was on deck, to avoid him, Isabel went down below and tried to read—she was reading *War and Peace*—but she knew she would never finish it. After a few pages she started to feel seasick and she had to shut the book. Lying on the bunk, Isabel would start picturing the middle-aged naked couple again. This time they were walking along a road in the dark—the woman was holding a palm leaf to her pubis, the man had cut his foot and was limping—when an old wooden truck rattled by. The old wooden truck came to a sudden stop. Several men were standing in the back of the truck; the men started to yell and hoot when they saw the naked couple. Frightened, the naked man and woman ran into the woods by the side of the road; yelling and hooting the men who were brandishing machetes and who were wearing shoes jumped off the truck and ran into the woods after them.

Once, on a particularly hot and airless afternoon, Isabel was down below taking a shower and washing her hair, when Neil opened the head door. Isabel was standing with her arms raised, her hands in her hair which was full of shampoo, and Neil held the door open and looked at her. They stood there without moving for at least a minute—the shower splashing out the door onto Neil's foot—until, at last, Neil shut the door.

When Neil said good-bye, he tried to kiss Isabel on the mouth but she turned her head at the last minute and he kissed Isabel's hair.

"I'll get you later, Isabel," Neil said.

After Neil left, Sam and Isabel sailed away the same day. They didn't want to stay in St. Thomas. Neither Sam nor Isabel spoke about Neil; they wanted to forget about him. Only at dinner that night, Isabel said, "You think that story about the man and woman swimming naked was true?"

Sam shrugged. "Why would he make something like that up?"

"He gave me the creeps," she said. Despite the heat, Isabel shivered.

That night Sam and Isabel made love as if they had not made love for a week—which was nearly true—for while Neil was on board, Sam and Isabel made love quickly, silently, as if afraid of being seen or heard. Now, they left the cabin door open and made all the noise they wanted to.

The next day Isabel found a soiled yellow cap with the logo of a hardware store on it that Neil had forgotten and she threw the cap overboard. The cap floated for a long time—each time it disappeared under a wave Isabel thought the cap had sunk and was gone for good, but then it surfaced again. She watched the cap until it disappeared from view.

"Guess who I ran into? You'll never guess." Sam's voice was far too loud for their apartment.

"Ssh, you'll wake up the baby," Isabel said. "Who?"

"Neil. Remember the guy who sailed with us to St. Thomas?"

The baby started to cry and Isabel didn't answer Sam.

The second house Sam and Isabel lived in was a third-floor walk-up off Kendall Square in Cambridge, Massachusetts. Sam was in business school and they had a baby; another baby was already on the way. The apartment was too small and whatever available space was filled with cribs, playpens, strollers, toys. Outside it was always raining or snowing and, alone with the baby all day, Isabel was lonely. Whenever the baby was sleeping, Isabel would lie down on their bed. If she tried to read—Isabel never finished *War and Peace* and she had switched to romances—she could not concentrate or remember what she had read. Often Sam came home late, after Isabel had eaten, and she left his dinner on top of the stove which he ate with a book lying open next to his plate.

The *Eudora* was in dry-dock in a boatyard near Sam's parents' summer house. Once or twice, Sam drove out by himself to sand and repaint her hull. They had not sailed her in over a year.

"Where did you run into him?" Isabel asked Sam after she had fed the baby.

Sam did not raise his head. "Who?"

"Neil. The guy from the Caribbean."

"In the Square. In a drugstore. He was buying a package of condoms."

"You're kidding," Isabel said. "And what were *you* buying?"

"Isabel, hey!"

Tired and fat, Isabel no longer wanted to make love. In bed, if Sam touched her, Isabel shrugged off his hand and turned away.

"Not now," she said.

"When?"

"I don't know. After the baby, maybe."

"Christ," Sam answered as he, too, turned away, "that's four months from now. Why don't you just say *never,* Isabel."

"Okay. Never."

The next day Neil telephoned. He must have gotten their telephone number from information, unless Sam had given it to him.

"Yeah, sure. Sure. That's great. Fine. Give me the address again," Isabel heard Sam say.

The party was in Boston, on Beacon Hill; Neil was house-sitting. A bar had been set up downstairs in the dining room and a lot of people Sam and Isabel did not know were milling around the antique oak table. Isabel got a glass of soda water, Sam got a beer and they went upstairs. When Neil saw them, he came right over.

"God, I'm glad to see you." He shook Sam's hand up and down. Again, he tried to kiss Isabel on the lips and Isabel ducked.

"God," Neil said again, "I love pregnant women. Pregnant women are so sexy."

"Jesus, Neil," Sam said, but he was laughing.

Neil came and sat down next to Isabel on the chintz-covered sofa. His hairline had receded and he no longer looked so boyish. "You know what? The first woman I ever made love to was pregnant," he told her. "The woman I lost my virginity to. She was ten years older than I was and I had the biggest crush on her."

"Neil. You're full of it," Isabel said.

"No. It's true. I swear. Her name was Elizabeth. She was gorgeous and she must have been seven months pregnant at least. She was out to here." Neil held his arms out like he was holding a huge beach ball. "Do me a favor, Isabel—can I touch your stomach?"

Looking around the room, Isabel once again heard his voice before she saw him. His back to her, Sam was standing across the room telling a woman with long blond hair a story—". . . first the father fell overboard then his son jumped overboard to try and save him, then the second son jumped overboard to try and save his father and brother, and finally the third son who was the only one left on the boat jumped overboard—"

The woman with the long blond hair was frowning and nodding, the corners of her mouth were turned down to show her distress.

The third house Sam and Isabel lived in was a small house in Westchester County. Every morning Sam took the train into the city to work in a bank while Isabel stayed at home and looked after the two little boys. Sam had brought the *Eudora* to a marina in nearby Rye, and, on weekends, weather permitting, Sam went sailing. Mostly, he sailed alone; one time he took the oldest little boy, Sam Junior, with him. Sam Junior was fair-skinned and small for his age and he was always sucking on something. On board the *Eudora,* Sam Junior had the nylon strap of his orange never-sink in his mouth.

Sam could never explain how it happened exactly except to say that it happened so fast and to say that when they came about and Sam Junior stood up to move from the windward side to the leeward side of the boat and he was still sucking on the strap of the never-sink, Sam shouted: "Will you take that goddamn strap out of your mouth!" at the same time as Sam tried to snatch the strap out of Sam Junior's mouth so that Sam Junior must have jerked away just as the boom swung over and hit him on the head. Without a sound, Sam Junior went overboard, and by the time Sam had jibed the boat and headed the boat into the wind and was able to grab his son out of the water, his son had drowned.

Years later and long after Sam sold the *Eudora* and after he and Isabel separated and Isabel is still living in the house in Westchester County with the one boy, she receives a postcard which has been forwarded to her—Isabel can hardly believe this—from her previous address in Massachusetts. The postcard is torn and mangled and it arrives in a plastic cover; the postmark is several months old and from the island of Barbados. The picture on the postcard is of a long white beach with palm trees and the message reads: *Wish you were here!;* it is signed *Love, Neil.* Isabel starts to throw the postcard away in the wastepaper basket when instead, for no reason she can think of, she looks at the picture again. The picture reminds her of something but she is not quite sure of what. Something that has stayed lodged in the back of her head, like a dream, and only later, a few hours later that same day when she is in the car on her way to pick up her son from school, does she remember what it is.

Isabel has remembered the story of the middle-aged naked couple who swam off the boat at night that Neil had told them about and how they could not get back on board and she also has remembered how she had told Neil that they could have swum to shore. Once again, as she drives her car, Isabel can picture the naked middle-aged couple swimming to the beach in the dark, then stumbling and shivering and walking to the house where there is still a light, only this time when the couple knock on the door and the dog barks, she pictures how the people who open the door to the house give the couple towels and how the dog stops barking. And after the couple have dried themselves off with the towels, Isabel pictures how the people who live in the house also give the couple some clothes—a pair of pants, a clean white shirt, a skirt, a red blouse, Isabel imagines—and after the couple are dressed and are patting the dog, how the people who live in the house fix them something to eat and bring them each a cup of hot tea and when the middle-aged couple are done eating and drinking, how the people who live in the house give them a place to sleep.

With gratitude and love to Robert Jones